I0537870

Love bad boy romances? Sign up for my no-spam mailing list to receive news on **new releases, free giveaways, and more!**

You can also join the advanced review team. I'm very much in need of people who are willing to read my books early and leave reviews upon release.

http://eepurl.com/bYD3Rv

CHAPTER 1: AXL

I killed my bike's engine as I slowed to a stop in the junkyard, pulling up alongside Ryker and Lynch. Behind them were ten or twelve guys on their bikes and the box truck that held our guns.

Everything was in place for the deal.

My bike's final rumble escaped into the scorched Arizona desert, echoing through the rows of dead, shredded cars. Then, the junkyard was quiet.

"Heat's fuckin' miserable," grunted Lynch, our road captain. He dipped his hand into a saddle bag and withdrew a silver canteen which he unscrewed and tipped against his lips. "Goddamn Reapers chose the most fucked up place ever for this deal."

He was right. I was drenched in sweat under my skullcap. My balls were boiling and every inch of exposed skin was frying in the sun. But it didn't fucking matter. Lynch should've known better than to bitch about the deal to his VP and President.

"Shut up, Lynch," I growled. As VP, I kept unruly Sons in line so Prez Ryker didn't have to. I led the men. Set the

1

example. And shut whiny little cunts right the fuck up. "Ryker says we do this, we do it. Selling our guns to Reapers gets my fuckin' goat too, but this ain't a choice."

"Bullshit," said Lynch, turning to face me. "We could've sold to the Colombians, not the enemy," he sneered.

His face was reddened and rough, his shaved head pockmarked with scars. His nose was visibly crooked, broken in God knows how many bar fights. Ryker, with his long graying hair and gaunt figure, was rough around the edges himself. But Lynch was a real ugly motherfucker.

My fists tensed and my teeth clenched. "Fall in line, Lynch," I said. I locked my eyes onto his, my expression deadly. He'd been this way ever since I made VP. Wanted the job himself and now thought I was keeping him on the outside. Well, he wasn't wrong. Only reason he was still breathing was 'cause Ryker owed him big time, but I wanted him out. Fucker was a wildcard and couldn't be trusted.

"Lynch, you got a problem, we'll settle up later," I said. "This ain't the time."

"VP's right," said Ryker. His voice drawled and had a hint of his Scottish accent. "Stay hard, stay sharp. This is a deal with the devil."

Lynch grunted. I wanted to hop off my bike and put a fist through his eye socket, but Ryker was right. We had to focus.

I listened for Reaper bikes, but there was only the howl of hot wind sweeping through twisted, trashed car frames. I looked down at my watch. Sixteen minutes after three already. The Reapers were definitely fucking with us, letting us sweat. And since we needed their money more than they needed our guns, there wasn't shit we could do about it.

2

Then, I heard their bikes and saw dust and exhaust rising from the opposite end of the junkyard. Didn't feel like an ambush to me. Little disappointing, can't lie. For a Son of Chaos like me born to fuck and fight, any lost opportunity to crack Reaper skulls was a damn shame.

The Reapers' bikes came into full view and rode toward us, down the center lane of the junkyard. About a dozen bikes and one box truck, just like our crew. Just like we agreed.

As they pulled closer, I recognized the lead rider. Tony Vargas, fat man extraordinaire and Reaper president.

Ask the guy to walk his own grammy across the street, next thing she knows she can't find her wallet. Or just ends up dead in an alley.

Vargas came to a stop ten yards in front of us, his guys pulling up behind him. He dismounted his bike, its suspension groaning in relief. Next to me, Ryker swung a lithe leg over his bike and dismounted. He stepped forward, catlike, his dark and white speckled ponytail swinging in the desert wind. "Vargas," he said grimly.

Vargas's face broke into a shit-eating grin. I had to fight back an urge to charge forward, seize his pudgy Reaper head, and mop the desert floor with his face.

"Long time no see, Larson," said Vargas. "You got the guns?"

Ryker stuck his thumb out and motioned toward the box truck. "Fifty AR rifles. Converted. Full auto sear in each one."

Vargas rubbed his fat hands together. "God, that makes me hard," he said. "You know, this could really be the start of something beautiful."

Ryker shook his head. "No chance. One time only. And these are for killing Mongols only. If we ever hear a fucking whisper about these guns in Sons territory-"

Vargas cut him off. His face broke into a sickly sweet, innocent smile and he turned his palms upward, shrugging. "Have some faith, Larson," he said, pointing to a gold cross that hung around his neck. "I'm a man," he said, "of my word."

"Cash," said Ryker, stiffly.

Vargas motioned to a patch who had a duffel bag hanging from his shoulder. But as the man stepped forward, a voice from the pack of Reapers cried out.

"Boss—in the pickup!"

All heads, Sons and Reapers, swiveled to an old, rusted-out red Ford truck sitting next to our box truck. What I saw made my chest pound. Inside the pickup truck was a young little thing who didn't look a day over 20. She was crouched down low behind the steering wheel, her shimmering black hair spilling over her shoulders.

She was holding—what looked to me—like a fucking video camera.

I had no idea how in the fuck she'd managed to sneak in there, or what she thought she was doing. Oh lord, was she dead. The two clubs would never let her out of here alive.

And that was just a real goddamn shame, because she was the most gorgeous woman I'd ever seen during my entire 28 years on this fucked-up Earth.

CHAPTER 2: HOLLY

I grew up in Bumfuck, Nowhere, an outskirt of an outskirt somewhere in the middle of Arizona. On a map it was called Coppertail, but it was the kind of town that even mapmakers forgot about.

In a town of rednecks and skeletons, I was the smart, shy girl. The one with a bright future, the first one to go to college. My parents and the local townsfolk projected their own unfulfilled hopes and dreams onto my future, as if it were my destiny to finally bring Coppertail its glorious dues. In a washed up old slum like that, my smarts almost made me a Z-list celebrity, which in Coppertail was a legitimate credential.

Probably the worst part of the town, aside from its isolation, was its lack of guys. I noticed it more and more as I grew up. The men were drunkards and gamblers and the boys followed in their footsteps.

My parents brought me up to be better than that. They wanted me to move to the city after college and marry a lawyer or a nice Jewish doctor. And that was... fine, I guessed.

But it wasn't exactly my fantasy. I mean, I was a nerd but I wasn't a total square. I really just wanted a gorgeous knight in shining armor to ride through Coppertail, sweep me off my feet, and take me away. I didn't think I was much to look at, but a girl can dream, right?

Of course, if that ever happened, my mom and dad would've been *"so"* disappointed in me for not "living up to my potential." Yeah, that was my parents. Always wanting me to make them happy, even if I sacrificed my own happiness in the process.

Anyway, no knight ever appeared to take me away. But my parents did well with their accounting business, well enough to eventually send me to Southern Arizona University without too many student loans. At SAU I met some guys and got a little experience, but they all faded into the background.

I did at least fall in love with something at SAU: photography and cinema. So I designed my own major that culminated in a senior documentary project, a video documentary of Coppertail. It was my baby, and maybe my way of saying goodbye to the town. I just knew I was gonna blow the lid off the national indie film festivals with my hot new release, and send my career into the stratosphere straight out of college.

At least, that was my plan until that Thursday afternoon when I went out to the old Coppertail junkyard with my new video camera. I had a great idea to use the junkyard to represent the spirit of Coppertail—some tumbleweeds blowing in the wind through a graveyard of old, torn up metal corpses.

I parked my car, a little Honda Civic with a long-broken odometer, outside the junkyard grounds. I'd heard that driving into the junkyard was a guaranteed flat, so I left it outside the perimeter and walked in.

I was filming next to an old red Ford pickup when I heard the unmistakable growl of loud motorcycle pipes. But it wasn't one bike, it was at least a dozen.

When they kept getting louder and louder, I got a weird feeling in my stomach. I always tried to follow my intuition, and my intuition told me to get out of sight. So I hopped into the truck and slouched down low. I kept my camera rolling, though, because that's the number one rule of video journalism. Soon a second motorcycle gang showed up, and it began to dawn on me that I was somewhere I really should not have been.

Unfortunately for me, I was far less stealthy than I'd thought, and the bikers spotted me easily. I almost threw up all over myself when one of the bikers shouted, "in the pickup!"

After the shout, there was confusion. Time paused while the stink of betrayal billowed over the scene. I didn't know much about motorcycle gang deals, but it didn't take an expert to figure out what was happening when the gunfire started: Each club thought I was working for the other. And as I found out, motorcycle gangs really don't like being spied on.

The only thing that saved my life was one biker—my knight in shining armor who I later came to know as Axl Archer—sprinting toward the pickup, diving in, and pinning my body down to the floor with his hard, muscled, tattooed, six-and-a-half foot body. It must've been the adrenaline, because even as I felt the shockwaves of bullets flying overhead, even as my video camera fell and shattered into pieces, all I could think about was how he instantly set my senses on fire.

"Who are you? Who fucking sent you?" he yelled over the gunshots. His elbow stabbed hard into my chest, pushing me against the Ford's crusty floorboards. His weight crushed the air out of my lungs and brought me back to reality. Anger and confusion seethed through his perfect teeth and through his soft-looking lips. Sweat plastered his thick, black hair over his forehead, and dripped down his square jaw into his dark beard. He was like a heartthrob actor, meticulously vetted for a movie role, costumed and made up by the best in the industry. Except it wasn't Hollywood, and he wasn't an actor. He was the man that Hollywood tries to mimic.

His stare penetrated me. And despite his anger, despite the violent scene unfolding outside, I don't know if I'd ever felt so safe and protected in my life as I did pinned beneath him. As if no one—nothing—could touch me.

"N-no one," I gasped, struggling to breathe. "I'm a-" I inhaled sharply, my lungs struggling to expand under this man's weight. Finally I succeeded, my windpipe wheezing. "-A film student," I puffed.

The biker's glare hardened, the muscles in his jaw popping out, his teeth gritting. He pressed his elbow even harder into my sternum, and I grimaced. Lying on my back on the truck floor, I could only see the clear blue afternoon sky through the truck's missing sunroof, but outside I heard yelling, screaming, and more gunshots. I could feel the adrenaline pumping through my bloodstream.

"Right," he spat, yelling over the commotion. "Don't they fucking teach you to stay out of other people's business?"

"Sorry," I croaked. "I-"

He cut me off by lowering his face to mine, our noses a fraction of an inch apart. His scent flooded my nostrils.

8

God... it was pure man. How could such a scruffy biker—a dangerous criminal—have this effect on me? And in these circumstances? I felt a strange distance, as if I were outside my own body looking in. This was bad. Seriously bad. What was I thinking?

"Do exactly as I fucking say," he hissed, "Or we're both dead."

I swallowed hard and nodded, feeling his breath on my lips as he spoke.

"I'm going-" The biker began to speak, but was interrupted by the driver's door at our feet swinging open. He twisted his body to look behind him, temporarily taking some of his weight off me. I craned my neck forward, lifting my head off the truck's floor to see what was happening. My stomach knotted as I saw a leather-clad figure looming just outside the truck, his gun raised, the barrel pointing straight down at us. The patch above the left breast pocket on his jacket said, "REAPERS."

My jaw dropped, a scream building up inside my chest. But before I could make a sound, the biker on top of me reacted. He sprung up, flipping onto his back and sitting up at the same time. His hand darted toward the gun faster than the Reaper could react, seizing the metal barrel and twisting the man's wrist backward until the barrel pointed directly into his own chest. There was a brief struggle, and then a deafening blast. A hot shell casing flew backwards and bounced off my arm, burning me and leaving a red welt. The Reaper's eyes rolled back into his head as his body collapsed into the desert sand outside the truck, his life taken from him.

The biker sitting on top of me—my protector—looked back at me over his shoulder. I gasped.

His handsome face was spattered with the blood of the dead Reaper.

Outside the truck, the gunshots were becoming less and less frequent. I tried to wiggle my legs out from under the biker to sit up, but he reached out with one powerful hand and pressed me backward, his hand over my breasts. He shook his head "No," and peered out of the truck. There was one more gunshot, some yelling, and then the roar of motorcycle engines.

He looked in my eyes again and nodded cautiously, taking his weight off me and carefully stepping out of the truck. I lifted myself onto the passenger bench, poking my head up just enough to see outside. But before I could process the scene, the biker reached back into the truck and pulled me out forcefully.

The clearing in the junkyard was now a scrambled mess of leather, metal, and bodies. There must have been five or six dead bikers, and it looked like a couple wore the same insignia as the one on my protector's jacket: SONS OF CHAOS.

I began to feel lightheaded, suddenly overwhelmed with the gravity of the situation. I sensed my protector, who was standing behind me, move closer. Another furious-looking, fat biker stormed toward me. "This bitch," he screamed, "is fucking dead!"

I'd never fainted before in my life, but I did this time, falling backward, my knees giving out. Before I blacked out, the last thing I felt were strong, warm arms encircling me from behind and breaking my fall.

CHAPTER 3: AXL

I saw that little spitfire's knees buckle and I caught her as she fell. My hands slid under her arms, my fingers feeling the soft but firm curves of her waist. Good fucking God, she felt so tender and precious in my hands. Her face was absolutely gorgeous. And there was something about her that I couldn't put my finger on.

...The fuck was my problem, anyway? If Axl Archer, VP of the Sons of Chaos and killer of men, was getting sentimental over a hot piece of ass that'd waltzed right into club business, then I'd well and truly fucking lost it.

I mean, shit, I'd been under a lot of pressure lately keeping the whole fucking club running smoothly. I couldn't rule out the possibility that I'd finally reached my limit, snapped, and gone utterly fucking nuts. In fact, it was the only explanation that made any sense. Because this wasn't like me. I didn't get worked up over pussy.

But when Lynch stormed toward us and reached out for the girl, I instinctively thrust my palm into his chest, knocking him backward and creating a barrier between us. She'd fucked up, but no way in hell was I gonna let a petulant little punk like Lynch put his hands on her. Jesus. Men of honor didn't beat up a girl. This was about principle. The electricity she sent through my body with every touch had nothing to do with it.

At least that's what I told myself.

"Back off," I barked at Lynch. He stepped forward again, driving his weight into my outstretched hand, a dangerous look in his eyes. My palm pressed back against his chest, locking us in place like two warring bucks. The girl hung like a rag doll in my other arm.

"This's fucked," growled Lynch, staring at me with glassy eyes. "Girl's an operative. A Reaper. A video camera. You gotta be fucking kidding me."

Around us, chaos festered. The junkyard sand was muddied with dark red streaks, and overhead the sun beat down harder than ever. I could see two or three patches still lying in the sand, motionless. Dash, my best buddy, was kneeling down next to one of them alongside our medic, Red. Looked like the newest prospect. Poor kid had only been 18. Shit. Only a year older than I was when Ryker had pulled me off the streets.

I cleared the thought from my head. We needed to fucking get out of here fast, before the ice showed up.

"Fucking bullshit she is," I said. "Scared her to death back in that truck. Not a Reaper." I shook my head, feeling her soft, precious weight against my hard chest and abs. She felt light as a summer cloud, her hair spilling over my bicep, stray strands pinched in the crook of my elbow.

Ryker's voice broke through the dull background roar. "Lynch! Get your fuckin' ass over here!" Lynch gave me one final hateful glare, then turned and jogged toward the sound of Ryker's voice.

Logically, Lynch was right. She could be a snitch. We couldn't rule it out and the whole situation was fucking weird. But I thought back to the truck—how one look at her had sucked all the air out of my lungs. There was no deception in her eyes. Those were honest eyes if I'd ever seen any.

Then, I felt her stir in my arms, and those beautiful eyes fluttered open. She met my gaze and a lump formed in my stomach. "Wha... What happened?"

"You passed out," I said. I wanted to brush her hair out of her eyes and examine her body for injuries. But then I saw the prospect being hauled up off the ground and toward the box truck. Damn. Just a kid. My neck twitched. "Guess you finally realized how much shit you're in," I finished.

She regained her footing, taking her weight off my arm. She stepped backward, away from me. "Damn," she said in a whisper, her eyes darting around nervously. She began to open her mouth again but was interrupted by Ryker, Lynch, and Dash walking up to us.

Ryker stepped close to her, his pointed leather boots aimed right at her like daggers. I bristled, waiting for him to speak.

He stared hard into her eyes, his thick silver and black ponytail blowing in the hot breeze. He spoke simply. "Explain yourself."

The girl swallowed hard. "I'm a film student."

"Name?"

"Holly... Brown."

Ryker stared at her hard, not speaking. Ryker was a good judge of character. He didn't become president of the Sons by making a habit of misreading people. My fists involuntarily clenched, but I wasn't gonna speak out of line. I wasn't like Lynch.

Finally, Ryker spoke again. "The ever-loving fuck were you doin' out here," he said, motioning toward Dash, who held the busted-up video camera, "with that thing? Hell of a strange coincidence."

Holly responded quietly. "Footage for my project." She added, "I hid when I saw you."

Lynch spoke up. "But you kept fucking rolling. Didn't you? Stuck your nose where it didn't belong."

She looked down at the ground, not replying.

"Boss," Lynch continued, speaking to Ryker but keeping his eyes locked onto Holly's, "Ain't no reason to take a chance on this broad. She came into the desert of her own volition. Let's take her a little deeper into it and leave 'er there."

Dash nodded. "She brought bloodshed upon the Sons. Willingly or not, it doesn't matter."

The muscles in my neck tightened. Leaving any innocent to die in the desert wasn't justice. And *especially* not her. Even a gun to my head at that moment couldn't have convinced me to do that.

Fortunately, it didn't come to that.

Ryker turned his head and looked at me. "What d'you think, VP?"

Holly was looking sidelong at me, her eyes anxious. I paused for a second of thought and then spoke. "Look, we gotta split. Cops could be here any minute. We don't got the time to figure this out now. But if she's a Reaper, we gotta know. We take her back to the clubhouse and figure it out later."

Ryker looked in my eyes and slowly nodded. "It's decided. We'll find the truth later."

I reached out toward Holly with my palm, everything a blur. She took my hand and I led her away from the other guys, Lynch seething. We got on my bike and we rode like hell away from that pit of death.

CHAPTER 4: HOLLY

My body sank into the cool sheets, surrendering to the weight of his tanned, muscled body. My nipples stiffened, aching for his touch. His kisses turned to bites, sneaking their way down my neck, and all my muscles clenched. My fingernails left their mark on his back as his thick, swollen manhood pressed against me through the elastic fabric of my sweatpants. I needed him inside me.

Then I woke up and I remembered everything.

The room was small and dark, and the walls were paneled with wood. Real wood, not imitation, and it had a rich veneer as if it'd been there for generations. Motorcycle memorabilia hung on the walls, leather clothing hung sloppily in the closet, and a large, faded Union flag hung over the window, darkening the room. Some light peeked through, but I'd lost all sense of time. I felt hidden, secluded, as if I were a secret not meant to be exposed. I must've been here overnight. When they'd left me, I'd fallen asleep fast, utterly drained from the heat and the chaos of the day.

But I ran my hands over my body, and I was in one piece. Whole.

I thought back to yesterday. The junkyard. The bikers. The total mayhem and how suddenly it'd all happened. It was crazy. 24 hours ago, I'd just been the same old brainiac Holly doing my thing. Now I was in some criminal biker's bed, mixed up in dangerous business that wasn't my own. Oh, and responsible for starting a deadly gunfight.

They say life can change in an instant, and mine sure had. But that wasn't the worst of it.

The worst part was how he—this criminal biker—had instantly made me feel something I'd never felt before. Some deep, fundamental attraction.

What the hell was wrong with me? After being taken by a strange and dangerous man on a motorcycle, you'd think escape would be my plan. But for some strange, stupid, and completely illogical reason, I felt a compulsion to get a little closer, to take in a little more of that indescribable feeling he gave me.

It made absolutely no sense. I'd read about Stockholm Syndrome, where prisoners become sympathetic to their captors. Was that my problem?

Whatever. I felt dumb. This was probably the same effect he had on all women, many of whom were far more gorgeous than I was. I was being ridiculous, wasting my brainpower on something that didn't even matter.

Then the door unlatched, interrupting my train of thought. My impossibly handsome captor stepped into the room, all burly shoulders, arms, muscle, tattoos, and jawline. He shut the door again behind him. I sat bolt upright in bed, instinctively pulling the covers over myself, even though I had slept in my clothes.

"Was startin' to think you'd never wake up," he said. His voice was gravelly and weary, his mouth a grim line. His thick black hair hung down over his forehead, annoyingly attractive for being so unkempt. Dark circles shaded the areas under his eyes. His broad shoulders were still covered by his black leather cut, the front lapel emblazoned with the club patch.

"How long have I been here?" I demanded.

His eyebrow rose, his eyes scanning me. "Since yesterday evening. It's past noon. Been up all night waitin' for you to wake the fuck up."

"Oh my god," I said, an acidic urgency permeating my stomach. "I should be in class right now." I patted around my jean pockets, feeling for my phone, but my pockets were empty.

He reached into his vest pocket and produced it. But instead of tossing it to me, he put it back in his pocket. "Sorry. Had to make sure you wouldn't call the cops."

It dawned on me that class might be on hold for a while. "I just want to go home," I said.

"Yeah," he said slowly, his brow furrowing. "Can't let you. Not yet."

A hotness welled up inside me. "Am I being kidnapped?" I said, looking into his eyes angrily. I couldn't believe the mess I was in.

"Wouldn't toss around accusations if I were you," he said, crossing his arms and staring straight into my eyes. "Without me, you might be rottin' in the desert right now."

"I told you," I said, shifting uncomfortably, "I don't know who you are and I don't care. I was filming for a class project. That's it."

"What the hell kind of project takes you to the middle of the fuckin' desert?" he asked.

"A documentary of Coppertail."

He scoffed. "Oh, of Coppertail. Great idea for a video."

"It's my home town," I said, feeling defensive. "You don't have to be a dick."

He stared at me for a moment and then erupted in laughter. "I didn't know they had people like you in Coppertail."

"What's that supposed to mean?" Why was he such a jerk?

"Nothing, darlin'," he said, a twinkle in his eyes. Then his expression turned serious and I noticed the weariness on his face again. "You'll get your chance to explain to the club tonight. Then you can get outta here, or do whatever. But right now I need some sleep."

"This is your room?" I asked incredulously.

"Yeah."

"So I've been sleeping in your bed?"

"Yeah," he smirked. "Lucky you, huh?"

Who did this asshole think he was? I was angry that my circumstances were so far out of my control. And that he was such a smug dick. And that despite everything, I couldn't take my eyes off him. At best, I guessed he might be generously willing to use me for a fuck before throwing me away. That's probably what his whole "darlin'" routine was about. Ugh.

"Gross," I said, but I had to force my face to make a convincing frown.

A faint flicker of a grin crossed his face. "Bullshit," he said.

"I don't even know your name."

"It's Axl. Axl Archer."

19

I opened my mouth to shoot back another smart-ass reply, but before I could, he said, "Just do something with yourself so I can catch some shut-eye."

I glanced around the room again. There was only a small desk with an uncomfortable-looking wooden chair. "I have to sit at that thing?"

He sighed, visibly annoyed. He shrugged off his cut, tossed it onto the desk, and bent over to unlace his boots. His sculpted shoulders and biceps bulged under his white undershirt. "I don't give a flying fuck. But I highly suggest not leaving this room if you know what's good for you."

I crossed my arms, annoyed, and scooted over to the very edge of the bed. I sat up against the backboard. "That enough space for you, princess?" I said.

He stared at me for a second, then chuckled under his breath. "Whatever, darlin'," he said, collapsing onto the opposite side of the bed. He turned away from me, lying on his side. He grabbed a pillow and tucked it under his head. "Don't wake me up."

I silently glared at the back of his head, my arms still crossed. After only two or three minutes, his back began to rise and fall regularly.

I didn't want to, but I thought back to my dream as I watched him lie an arm's length away from me. The feeling of him on top of me, claiming me, about to fill me up.

I wanted it so bad. And that *really* pissed me off.

CHAPTER 5: AXL

When I finally woke up, it was pitch black outside. I'd slept all day since passing out at noon. Good. That's how I fucking liked it. My kind of schedule.

No light came through the cracks of the window. My head throbbed, pounding from a concoction of violence, booze, and sleep deprivation. It'd been a long night at the bar downstairs while Holly slept in my bed. I always heard that civilians slept like the dead after seeing club shit go down—just 'cause of pure adrenaline. I guess it was true, 'cause she'd been out for almost 18 hours. Me, I could drink it off, but not everybody's got the stomach for this shit.

So yeah, she'd been in my bed, and goddamn was she gorgeous. I didn't know what'd possessed me to allow it, though. I didn't just let furniture crash in my bed for the night. They put out and then got out. Those were the rules and every club slut knew them.

But fuck, there was just something about Holly. It wasn't just her tight body teasing me, getting my gears turning. There was something else. Something in the way she

21

carried herself, something about the quiet confidence. Civvies usually turned into a blubbering fuckin' mess in a position like this. But she held it together. And there was something under that shyness that suggested a kind soul.

And that was worth something to me. I mean, shit, ever since Ryker had gotten me off the streets and into the club, I'd done some fucked up shit. To people that deserved it, of course. But Holly didn't seem capable of that garbage, and that refreshed me. Even I could appreciate a woman who didn't stoop down to the club lifestyle. Not like the hanger-on and beggar sluts that came and went.

Or maybe none of that was true, and I was just another horny piece of shit.

Nah. There *was* something about her.

I rubbed my eyes and flipped onto my back. A dull glow came from the corner of the room. Holly sat at my desk, the lamplight on, her legs pulled up to her chest as if to isolate herself from her surroundings. On the desk was her phone and she was poking at it. She must've heard me stir, because she turned toward me, her face angry as the devil's.

"You changed the passcode," she said hotly.

I grimaced, my temples on fire. It was too fucking early to get sassed. Shit just never fucking ended around here. "Already told you," I said, "You gotta lay low while we deal with this."

"I need to call my roommates. They're probably worried to death."

"Thought college was about independence," I groaned, shutting my eyes and applying pressure to my forehead.

"I went into the desert and didn't come back. They're gonna be worried. What do you know about college, anyway?"

I chuckled. "A college degree don't do much for you in this lifestyle, darlin'. Don't remember a spot for that on the club application."

"Shocking."

I got out of bed, stretching my muscles. I caught Holly staring out of the corner of my eye as I grabbed a bottle of aspirin from the dresser. She stood up and walked over to me, holding out her phone.

"You said I'm not being kidnapped. So let me text them."

I thought for a minute and groaned. "Give it to me," I said. She handed over the phone and I unlocked it.

"What am I supposed to say, anyway?"

"That you're fine. Not to worry."

She eyed me. "Will I be fine?"

You'll be more than fine if I have my way with you.

"Everyone wants this to blow over as fast as possible."

I watched her text her roommates and dial her parents, ready to snatch the phone out of her hands if she called the heat. But she played by the rules. When she hung up, I held out my hand.

She handed over her phone again with a scowl, and as she did so, our hands touched. She didn't withdraw, though. Energy seared through me like a solar ray.

Maybe I really was losing my fucking mind. I didn't understand why she had this effect on me, and I didn't like that. It was fucking dangerous.

I stepped closer to her, her knees touching my legs. She looked up into my eyes, her expression suddenly shy. But I knew it wasn't the fucking time to make a move on this chick. She'd slopped enough shit on our plates already, and part of me felt like it'd just be a damn shame if any of my scumbaggery rubbed off on her. Not that I knew it'd work anyway. Yeah, she couldn't help staring at me, but that didn't really mean shit. She probably hated my guts for keeping her here.

Breaking our gaze and stepping away from her, I took the phone from her fingers and hit the lock button. The screen powered off with a click.

I sat down on the edge of the bed and grabbed my boots, pulling them onto my feet and lacing them up. I looked at the clock: 7:29pm. "Club meeting at eight," I said. "We'll figure out what happens to you then."

"And what do I do until then?"

"Stay here," I said. "And don't fucking leave until I come back."

I walked to the door, opened it, and slipped out of the room. I needed a fucking reality check, and I was going to get it.

I thundered down the stairs to the clubhouse common room, where the bar and pool table were. At least a dozen guys were mingling there, already waiting for the meeting. My buddy Dash caught my eye. Dash was my bro. He'd been with me through thick and thin, ever since the beginning. He'd saved my ass on more than a few occasions.

"Yo, VP, how was she?" A couple other guys looked over and snickered.

Normally I'd have laughed it up with the guys. But with this chick it just pissed me off for some reason.

I shook my head. "Didn't take advantage of her, I'm not a fuckin' brute," I said. "And don't say another fucking word about that girl."

The guys stared, their expressions shellshocked.

I walked over to the bar where I recognized a blonde with big tits that I'd hooked up with before. She was sitting with another piece of furniture. Couldn't remember her name, but I slung my arm around her shoulder.

"Hey doll," I said, putting on my winning grin, "Something's going on with the pipes... downstairs. Need you to come take a closer look."

She grinned back at me, proud to have been singled out by the club VP, understanding my intentions. "Hey Axl honey," she said, "I'm an expert plumber. Just show me where the problem is."

I held her hand as she got off the barstool, and took her into a curtained-off side room that we called the VIP room. I unzipped my jeans and took out my thick, veiny cock. She dropped to her knees and took it in her mouth, tonguing me with years of experience. But she sucked and sucked, and I just wasn't feeling it. All I could think about was that little spitfire in my room. I shut my eyes, imagining it was Holly, and then—only then—did I start to get into it.

But a moment later I was interrupted by someone ripping the curtains aside.

It was Holly. She looked at the scene in front of her, then shook her head, turned around and stomped toward the club exit.

CHAPTER 6: HOLLY

When Axl left the room, I was scared and angry. Scared to be going on trial in front of a gang of motorcycle-riding thugs and killers. Angry that I was a prisoner in this tiny, dark room, my every move being watched and controlled.

But even worse, I was angry at my heart for beating out of my chest every time I touched him. I mean... honestly. He may have been handsome, but how different could he really be from the loser drunkards that populated Coppertail? He was nothing but a more handsome version of them.

My best course of action would be to explain everything to Ryker and the club—yet again—clear my name, get out of here as fast as possible, and put this all behind me. I shuddered to think what would happen if my parents found out about this.

In my head, a vision played of me introducing Axl to my parents and—God, what a ridiculous notion. Not only was I developing an idiot crush on a criminal, I was becoming delusional. As if he'd ever use me for anything more than a fuck.

After he left me alone, I sat stewing on the hard, uncomfortable wooden chair until I'd had enough. I was going downstairs, finding Axl, and demanding that we get this "meeting" underway. If I was going to die, I might as well get it over with as soon as possible.

I stormed down the stairs into the main clubhouse, a large open area with a high, peaked wooden ceiling. On one side of the room there was a long bar, and on the other side there were various tables and booths, as well as a pinball machine and a couple sofas. There were at least two dozen bikers milling around, drinking. As soon as I entered, it felt like all heads turned to me. There was a lot of snickering. I felt my face redden.

"Where's Axl?" I demanded of a fat, leather-clad biker with a round face. He laughed at me, showing his yellow teeth, and pointed at a closet behind the bar area. I stormed over to the closet and threw the curtain open.

Knowing that I shouldn't care made it that much worse when I saw Axl in the closet. The blonde bimbo was on her knees in front of him, with his jeans unzipped and his huge, thick cock in her mouth.

It wasn't my business, and I had no right to be upset. It wasn't like I'd walked in on a cheating husband or boyfriend. Axl Archer was the absolute furthest thing from my boyfriend that a guy could get. And that only made it worse. It was just plain, ugly jealousy, and it was completely in spite of myself. Of course an asshole like him would be into big-titted blondes.

They both looked at me in surprise when I threw the door open. "What the hell?" said Axl. "Do you *always* butt into other people's business?"

I put my hands on my hips, ready to reply, but uproarious laughter from the bikers behind me drowned out my thoughts. Instead of replying, I slammed the curtain shut in that asshole's face, turned around, and stomped through the crowd of laughing bikers. I beelined for the main club exit, and walked right out into the night. I expected someone to come out and grab me, but no one did. Apparently leaving was as easy as just walking out.

The outside night air was cool and refreshing, a stark change from the afternoon heat. Looking around, I realized that the clubhouse was totally isolated. The property was surrounded by an iron cattle fence. Just outside the fence was a roughly paved road that looked like it ran two or three miles into a small town. I decided to follow it. Since nobody had stopped me, I was getting the hell out of here and going home myself. They could keep my phone, and I'd deal with my car later. Axl and the rest of the bikers would have to figure out their own problems. I wasn't part of it. I didn't even have the footage from the junkyard, if that was what they were so worried about. I was through with this crap.

I crossed the property's perimeter and starting walking toward the town, its lights shining like stars in the distance.

Of course, I should've known it wouldn't be that easy. I'd barely gotten a quarter mile down the road when I heard the deep rumble of a motorcycle engine behind me. I thought about running, or screaming and hoping that a passerby would hear, but I thought better of it. As the rumble grew closer, the bike's headlight flooded the road ahead of me in light. I stopped my march and whirled around. It was Axl, on his bike—of course. He slowed his bike to a stop, flipped out the kickstand with his foot, and dismounted. He hadn't bothered to put his helmet on, and his raven black hair was tousled back by the wind. His irises sparkled like stars, and his eyes crinkled at the corners as he chuckled at me.

"What the hell?" I demanded. "Go get your dick sucked some more. I had nothing to do with this, so let me go!"

"Darlin'," he said, chuckling, "You're pretty cute when you're mad."

Anger swelled up inside me. "This isn't a fucking joke. This is kidnapping!" And he was calling me cute? What the hell? Was I being punked?

His grin faded and his expression turned serious. He cleared his throat. "Look," he said, "I know you ain't a Reaper. And I'll do what I can to get you outta this jam. But understand me, you got blood on your hands now. You gotta play by our rules. You gotta answer our questions if you wanna get out of here. I wish it were my choice, but it ain't."

I suddenly felt scared again. Blood on my hands... Hearing it out loud made it feel real. Very real.

"You'd take me home if it were up to you?" I asked.

He hesitated briefly. "Eventually."

"What's that supposed to mean?"

He stepped closer to me, his body pressing up against mine. "After I take what I want," he said.

My heart started beating hard in my chest. Was he really making a move on me? Was I being stupid for letting him? "What's that?" I whispered.

His hands found my hips, then wandered to my back. He slipped one hand down to my ass, grabbing it hard, while his lips found mine. He kissed me lustfully.

Me? Little old Holly is what he wanted? My better judgment told me to turn my head and push him away.

But I didn't. I couldn't. He felt so good, tasted so good, and all I could do was surrender myself to him. I threw caution to the wind, didn't care if I was being slutty. I wanted to try something dirty.

If he wanted to use me, I'd use him right back.

CHAPTER 7: AXL

I stood on the side of the dark road, my bike's engine still rumbling. I wanted to forget this chick, to put her out of my mind and get her the hell out of our clubhouse. She didn't belong here.

But when I opened my mouth to say the words, my lips were concrete. When I tried to force myself to throw her on the back of my bike to haul her back to the clubhouse, my muscles were lead, my joints locked gears.

The club wanted this chick gone, but I couldn't stop thinking about her.

So when I looked into her beautiful brown eyes, reflecting the soft moonlight, I couldn't resist any longer.

I wrapped my hands around her waist, the curves of her body igniting my senses like napalm. My hands slid down to her ass, her skin separated from mine only by the thin fabric of her jeans. I hungered for her body, lusted after her delicate scent which hadn't left my mind since I first crashed into her in the truck cabin.

I squeezed hard and pulled her into me, pressing my lips against her lips. She gasped as our skin touched, welcoming my tongue against hers. Her smell instantly flooded my senses. Shit, I didn't know much about biology, but I'd been through enough club sluts to know that this attraction went deeper. It was instinctual, fundamental, ancient. And that scared the shit out of me, so I tried not to think about it as our tongues tangled and my hands wandered over her body freely.

When our lips parted at last, she pulled back and looked up at me with hungry eyes. "What the hell is this? What do you want from me?" she whispered.

Fuck. What didn't I want from her? I wanted to bend her over my bike, to take her right here, to mark her as mine and discover all her deepest secrets. After that, I didn't know. I didn't want to think about emotional shit right now. And no way in hell was I going to let onto any of this. But fuck yeah, there was something I wanted right now.

"Suck me, beautiful," I said, my voice husky with need. I brought a hand up to her cheek, savoring the softness of her skin against my rough, calloused, guilty hands. My fingers slipped behind her neck, intertwining with her thick, shiny hair. I gently—but firmly—pressed her down to her knees. She obeyed, and my hard cock stiffened even further at her show of obedience. This good girl knew how to take an order—at least when it involved the prospect of my cock. Yeah, I'd noticed how her eyes had been glued to it back at the club.

She sank down to her knees, running her hands down my six pack. Then she brought her hands lower, over my belt, letting her long nails scrape against my thick Kevlar riding jeans. She teased my cock through the fabric, driving me crazy with lust. Her hands continued down past my cock, exploring my rock-hard thighs, strengthened by years of holding my body tight against my bike.

She looked up at me, needful urgency in her eyes. "Help me take it out."

I chuckled to myself. Chicks were always intimidated by the belt buckle.

I unfastened my belt and then my jeans. She rubbed her hands against my thighs, impatient, just like I was. I unzipped my jeans and took her hand in mine. I placed it over the hard bulge beneath my boxers, and my erection stiffened against the palm of her hand.

"Axl," she gasped. She hooked her fingers over the elastic waistband of my boxers and gently pulled the waistband down. I felt the roughness of the fabric travel down the length of my hard shaft, revealing my erect manhood to her.

She wrapped her palm around the base of it, its girth too great for her fingertips to meet her thumb. She placed her other palm lightly on the shaft—barely enough to make contact—and ran it up and down the full length.

"God," I said, "This is all I've been able to fucking think about since I first saw you."

"Me too," she whispered. "God, I can't believe I'm doing this." The tone of her voice was one of guilty, lustful admission.

I looked intently into her eyes as her hands explored the new sensation of my cock. "Put it in your mouth. Now." I commanded her.

She did as she was told. She rubbed the sensitive underside against her soft lips. Then, she flicked her tongue over the tip, wetting it with her saliva.

"Oh, fuck," I said. My heat beat faster inside my chest, while my bike's engine rumbled steadily in the background.

33

Her tongue glided up and down my cock. I could feel it travel over the hard, thick, engorged veins. Then, she took the tip completely in her mouth. I felt her lips struggle and stretch to accommodate my girth, and I might have felt sorry for her taking on my monstrous dick. That is, if she didn't look like she was enjoying it so damn much.

She began to work up a rhythm with her mouth and hands, one hand on my balls and the other working up and down the length of my shaft, lubricated by the saliva of her precious mouth. She'd definitely done this before. I felt pressure building up in my balls, and I knew I wasn't going to last long. I reached down, running a hand through her hair, the sensuality of the moment heightening my arousal.

Holly looked up at me, taking her mouth off of me just long enough to ask, "Are you going to do it?"

"Oh, fuck yeah," I said, and pressed her head closer, pushing my cock deep into her throat.

She increased her pace and intensity, and pushed me over the edge.

"Oh, fuck," I grunted.

CHAPTER 8: HOLLY

My panties were dripping wet as I knelt on the side of the dirt road, the cool night breeze surrounding us, Axl Archer's huge cock filling up my mouth.

This made no sense whatsoever. He was bad for me. Bad, even though there was something more to him than the other bikers. Bad, even though my visceral attraction to him was stronger than anything I'd ever experienced before. Bad, even though for some reason I sensed a goodness inside him.

I should've kept running when I heard his bike behind me. I should've screamed until someone heard me and he was forced to let me go.

But I hadn't done that, because I couldn't resist him. Every sinew of his muscles, every hair that formed the handsome beard on his face, every aspect of his leathery, masculine scent—they all conspired against me and controlled me like a puppet. He was such a man, and he made me feel like a woman in a way that no other guy ever had.

Did he really find me beautiful? I knew I shouldn't care. But damn, it excited me to think that I had the same effect on him that he did on me.

So here I was, servicing this dirty biker's cock on the side of the road, in the middle of the night, and I loved every second of it.

When he started to come in my mouth, I ached with a need for him to fill me. I wanted to take him inside me, to feel everything he had to offer. He wasn't salty, wasn't bitter. Just sweet and sticky, and it satisfied me deeply as I swallowed him hungrily, not knowing when—or if—this would ever happen again. Even if this was destined to be a one-night stand—which it had better be—I wanted to savor every second of it.

He ran his hands through my hair again, and for a brief moment, they lingered. Then he quickly removed his hands, almost as if he'd caught himself doing something he shouldn't. He grabbed his cock, softer than before but still incredibly long and thick, and tucked it back inside his boxers as I stood up.

But now, there seemed to be a distance between us. The look on his face, which had been one of intense pleasure, changed to one of disapproval. The moment of intimacy— if you could even call it that—had passed.

Back to being a fucking asshole as soon as he got what he wanted. I should've known.

He looked at me hard. "Do you have any idea how much bullshit you've caused?" he asked. "If the club gets the idea that you're not under control, they just might take matters into their own hands."

My face flushed and felt hot. I could still taste him. "I'm not under your control," I said.

"Look," Axl said, "'Til Ryker gives the word, you're implicated in this."

"When's that going to happen?"

"Tonight. Like I told you. Probably be on your way already, if you hadn't had this genius idea."

I paused. "So you're saying this shouldn't have happened?"

He coughed. "I'm sayin' you shouldn't have run. Look. We gotta get back to the clubhouse and you'll be floating outta here like Mary Poppins in no time."

"Fine," I said. I wasn't about to show this asshole exactly how conflicted that actually made me feel. Hell, I wasn't even about to admit it to myself.

He unclipped the spare helmet from the back of his bike and handed it to me. I pulled it over my head, and then felt his fingers against my jaw as he moved to adjust the strap. "I know how," I said, twisting my head away from his hands. I reached up and succeeded in pulling the strap tight.

A surprised smile came over his face. "Huh," he said, "Guess you're a natural."

We rode back to the clubhouse on his bike, my hands wrapped around his torso. I could feel his hard abs through the t-shirt under his open leather jacket. But hell if I was going to cop a feel and give him anything else to feel cocky about.

When we got back to the club, we walked through the same door that I'd run out of. I followed Axl into the main room. It had reached a critical mass of bikers, and my little stunt had kept them all waiting. I went in expecting more crude jokes and wolf whistles—or worse—but instead we were greeted with cold, hard stares. I swallowed hard.

"Boss!" shouted a voice from the crowd. "VP's back. He's got the gash with him."

I bristled at the biker's language. It was fucking disgusting, but I didn't dare talk back.

On the side wall opposite the bar, one of two French double doors swung open, revealing what must've been the club office. Ryker emerged from the doors. A wave of agitated apprehension swirled around the room as he made his way through the crowd of bikers and lithely hopped up onto the bar counter. He stood tall, towering over the crowd. I couldn't help but feel my eyes be drawn to him. There was something about him, a charisma that made me understand why he'd become the leader of this club.

"Boys," he roared in his Scottish accent, "I know you're jonesing to hear the full story of the Reaper incident." A murmur ran through the crowd.

"As you know, this lovely lady," he said, gesturing at me, "found herself in a compromising position during our deal with Vargas. Decided she'd capture our smiling faces on her video camera. Caused a big ruckus." Even from the rear of the room where I stood, I could feel the daggers shooting at me from his eyes. "We proceeded under the assumption that she could be an operative. But we've verified with the appropriate channels, and she's clear."

A nervous sensation zapped through my belly. Had they talked to my school? My parents? Had they gone to my house? I looked up at Axl who stood next to me. "What does that mean?"

"Club has connections," he said. "Background checks for when we need to... know things. Don't worry about it."

His answer didn't ease my mind at all, but Ryker had begun speaking again.

"The Sons of Chaos do not harm innocents," he said, and then his eyes locked onto mine again. "But you had better fucking learn your lesson."

Bikers around the room cast sidelong glances at me, grumbling insults and swears. I swallowed hard, wondering if I should apologize. Next to me, Axl seemed to sense that I might speak. He gently elbowed me to get my attention, and I saw him shaking his head "no" out of the corner of my eye.

"But boys, make no mistake," continued Ryker. "Shit has been a long time coming with the Reapers, and this has only hastened it. Blood has been spilled. The Sons don't start wars, but we sure as hell end them. Watch your backs. Watch each other's backs. And prepare yourselves for what may come."

CHAPTER 9: AXL

When Ryker finished his speech and jumped down from the bar, a hot, agitated energy filled the room. Guys milled around, chatting in low tones. Instead of beers, the bartender was pouring hard liquor.

As club VP, I'd seen it all before. This was how guys acted at the prospect of war.

I turned to face Holly and she looked at me nervously. I knew she felt responsible for what Ryker had just said. "Axl," she said, "You have to believe me that I—"

I shrugged my shoulders, cutting her off, my expression blank. "Would've happened anyway," I said. "Shit's been heating up for months. Spark could've come at any time."

She looked distraught. "What does this mean for me?"

I studied her face hard. Her shiny black hair was pulled back into a ponytail, her bangs spilling down over her forehead. Her supple, young tits rose and fell under her shirt, the outline of her taut figure visible under the thin cotton fabric. I couldn't stop fucking thinking about earlier. How her body had felt against mine. How hard she'd made me when I grabbed her ass. How hard she'd made me come when she sucked me off. God, I'd never felt that before and I wanted more. I wanted to know what made her the way she was. But it couldn't happen. The guys already thought I was going soft over a gash. I had to put the club first and get her outta here.

My jaw clenched and my eye twitched. "It means you need to get the hell outta here."

"I know," she said, looking down at her feet. "So that's it?"

Hot acid burned in my stomach. Was she asking to see me again? She couldn't be fucking serious. Not like it mattered anyway. She'd never be welcome—or safe—around here. "You're going home, darlin'," I said, forcing myself to grin. "Come on. Let's go."

We headed outside, and guys got out of our way as we walked. They hadn't fucking forgotten who was in charge around here.

It was getting close to midnight, and outside a chill had come over the desert. Holly shivered as we walked to the bikes, which were parked in a line outside the garage. I felt a little fucking sorry for her, I guess.

"It's freezing," she said "You could offer me your jacket, you know."

I stopped in my tracks, swiveling to look her in the eyes. "You suck my cock once and you think you can wear a Sons patch? Fucking unbelievable."

"You know," she said, "you're a real dick."

I realized she didn't know what she'd asked for. She was just a civilian, not even a hanger-on. Gruffly, I added, "There's a sweatshirt in my saddlebag. Come on."

We walked the rest of the way to the bikes in silence, and I grabbed the sweatshirt for her. She put it on, before grabbing the passenger helmet off the back of my bike herself. She put it on and tightened it without my help and mounted the bike.

I swung onto the bike and started it. "Take me to my parents' house in Coppertail. Sabino and McClellan," she said.

We hit the road, leaving the club's hometown of Redstone. As soon as the bike's tires hit pavement, I twisted the throttle back and we thundered through the night.

When we pulled up to the intersection of Sabino and McClellan, she nudged me from behind to direct me to her house. During the ride, she'd buried her hands beneath my jacket, hanging on to my body underneath the leather. Just the feeling of those hands on my torso made my cock rock hard. Fucking pity we were on our way to her parents' place.

She guided me down a series of crappy-looking side streets until we finally pulled up in front of a small two-story house. Even at night, I could see that the property was well-maintained. A landscaped yard, a freshly painted house. Not like most houses in Coppertail.

I dismounted the bike first to let her off. She dismounted, then started to pull the sweatshirt over her head before pausing to ask, "Do you want this back?"

"Keep it," I said, wondering why she'd want that old piece of shit. I sighed. "You should put this all behind you as soon as possible."

She frowned, but there was a hint of... something on her face. Was it disappointment?

"At least be a gentleman and walk me to the door."

"What am I, a high school kid dropping you off before midnight?" My eyes rolled involuntarily. "Fine," I said, and dismounted the bike again.

We walked up the sidewalk to the door. I pulled her phone out of my pocket and held it out to her. "Oh yeah, don't forget this," I said. "The code's 1234."

She rolled her eyes at me.

"What?" I said.

She pulled a key out of the pocket of her jeans and began to insert it into the lock when suddenly the door swung open. In front of us was a middle-aged guy who looked like he did a lot of overtime at the office.

"Holly!" he said. "What are you doing here at this time of night—" He paused in mid-sentence and looked at me, his eyes scanning me and finally fixating on the Sons patch on my jacket's lapel. The look of disapproval on his face hardened. "Who the hell is this treasure?"

His words didn't bother me. I'd been called far worse. But I knew the best way to deal with these situations—by showing class. I spoke up before she had a chance to.

"Sir," I said, "Just an acquaintance of your daughter. Gave her a ride since her car broke down."

"Your car broke down?" he said, looking hard at Holly. "When were you planning to tell us about that?"

She sighed. "Dad, I'll tell you about it later."

"I better be on my way," I said.

Her father shifted his attention back to me. "I think that's a good idea."

I nodded solemnly, first at him, and then at Holly. "See you around," I said to her. She held my gaze until I pried my eyes away, turned around, and walked back to my bike.

When I got back to the clubhouse, I needed something. What exactly, I didn't know. I had the bartender pour me a double whiskey, but it left me unsatisfied. To fight or fuck. That's what I needed.

I hung out at the bar for fifteen or twenty minutes, drinking and wishing that some dumbass would come and cross me, but it didn't happen. With that off the table, there was only one option. So I chatted up a broad, a new hanger-on that I'd seen around the club lately. I hadn't hooked up with her yet, but she hadn't exactly been shy about checking me out.

Twenty minutes later, we were in my bed. She had her shirt off and I was sucking her huge tits, but I was barely paying attention. I couldn't take my mind off of Holly. Fuck. I needed to get my shit straight, and fast. But before I could get my dick wet, there was an urgent pounding at the door. A voice spoke up.

"VP! We've got a visitor."

"Tell them to fucking wait," I shot back. "I'm busy."

"It's important."

My teeth clenched and my hands balled up into fists. This was getting fucking ridiculous. But on the plus side, my dream of flattening someone's face tonight was about to come true.

"I'll be back," I said to the bimbo in my bed. "Stay here."

I pulled on my shirt, opened the door, and stormed out of the room.

It was almost three in the morning now, but downstairs was still buzzing. It looked like a fight was about to break out by the front door. It only took me a second to figure out why. Our little visitor was a fucking Reaper.

I stormed across the room, my footsteps echoing loudly. "Move!" I barked. I shoved guys aside, until I was face-to-face with the Reaper. I looked right into his eyes.

"Talk," I said with clenched teeth. I wanted to paint the walls with the blood in his brain, but I held myself back. Killing a messenger was a quick path to an all-out war.

"Message for your president," he said.

"In the middle of the night. You've gotta be fucking kidding me."

"Not my choice."

"We're not fucking bothering Ryker right now. Give it to me."

He looked around at the guys around me. I could see the nervousness under the surface.

"The girl," he said. "We're taking her out. Courtesy notice."

My blood boiled. I should've played it cool but my instincts were taking over. "She had nothing to do with this," I growled. "I know that. You fucking know that."

He shrugged, his body language betraying nervousness. "Not my choice," he said again. "She saw shit."

I growled again. "She's not what you want. You want the tape."

The Reaper looked me up and down. "She your old lady or something?"

I knew that the guys around me were asking themselves the same question.

"She ain't my old lady. She's an innocent. The tape," I repeated. "Leave her the hell out of this and we'll talk about the tape."

"Vargas also wants the tape. We'll come for that too. But the girl dies. It's about sending a message."

There was no point in arguing with this fuck. He was just a peon. And the Reapers were testing us, pushing our buttons. It was a provocation.

"Get out of my fucking club," I said coldly, without breaking eye contact.

The Reaper turned around and slipped through the door without a word. Outside, there was the sound of a bike starting up and pulling away.

"Fucking Reaper trash," said a voice behind me. "The fucking girl deserves it," said another voice angrily. A commotion of insults and arguments erupted, but it all faded into a blur in my head.

I could only think about one thing. I had to get to her before they did. But before I could react, Ryker's voice boomed out over the room.

"What in the ever-loving fuck is going on?"

CHAPTER 10: HOLLY

I was disoriented when I woke up on Saturday morning. I looked around, expecting to see the wood paneling and motorcycle memorabilia that hung on Axl's wall. But instead of wood paneling, there was only the baby blue wallpaper of my room at my parents' house. And instead of the Sons of Chaos club insignia, there was my favorite Georgia O'Keeffe painting, a reproduction that my parents had gotten me as my high school graduation gift almost four years ago.

Four years. I couldn't believe it had been that long. Four years and here I was, almost ready to graduate and jump into the real world. I thought for a moment, realizing how lucky I really was to be back home in my own bed. Things could've gone worse at the clubhouse. Much worse.

Light streamed in through my bedroom window, and it must have been noon already. I was still exhausted from the ordeal of the last two days, but for some reason I couldn't fall asleep again. Annoyed with my racing mind, I got out of bed and stretched. I needed to catch up on all the schoolwork I'd missed. And I needed to get my car back, and then there was the matter of my documentary. Now I had no footage and no camera. That was a real setback—an expensive one, too—but I'd figure it out.

Trying to push my concerns out of my mind, I swung my door open and headed downstairs to the kitchen. I realized I'd barely eaten anything at the clubhouse, and I was starving.

But when I walked into the kitchen, I stopped short. Both of my parents were sitting at the kitchen table, and it looked as if they'd hardly been speaking. I'd expected my dad to be in the garage, working on his project car like a usual Saturday, and my mom to be reading on the porch. But I could tell by their expressions that we were going to have a "talk."

My dad looked up from the coffee mug he was clasping between his hands on the table. "Afternoon, Holly," he said, his voice serious.

"Hi Dad," I said.

My mom spoke up. "Honey, we're worried about you. We talked to your roommates and they said you were gone for two days."

"And then you came back with that lowlife on a motorcycle. And your car is nowhere to be found," added my dad.

I sighed heavily. "I can explain the car," I said. "But I'm not a kid anymore. This is none of your business."

"Sit down," my father said sternly.

My mother nodded, the thinnest of veiled expressions covering the disappointment on her face.

I sighed again, pulled out a chair, and sat.

"Honey," my mom said, "We give you a lot of freedom. We want you to succeed. We really do. But we worry when you come home on the back of a motorcycle without your car. You should have come to us if you had a breakdown."

"I would've called you," I said. "I was down at the Coppertail junkyard filming for my capstone project. It wouldn't start, but Axl and a couple of his friends happened to come by and gave me a lift. It was fine."

My dad's eyebrow rose and he eyed me suspiciously. "So that's what you've been doing for the last two days? Hanging out with that lowlife and skipping class?" He drew quotation marks in the air with his fingers when he said "hanging out."

"It's not like that," I said. I felt a guilty pang in my stomach, but there was no way in hell I could tell my parents the truth, that I'd ignited a gang war, nearly got shot, and then hooked up with a criminal. That was so far away from their dream of me meeting a Jewish doctor that I might as well slap them both in the face.

"They just gave me a lift and took me to Brooke's place. I've been working nonstop with her on the documentary," I lied. "But last night I realized I forgot my keys at Axl's place. He brought them to me and then took me home. That's it," I said. "He looks rough but he's not a bad guy."

"Hol," my dad said. "We thought you were on the right track. Well, as much as you could be." I knew he was talking about my dream of becoming a filmmaker. It wasn't good enough for them, not as reliable as becoming a housewife or getting some kind of desk job where I'd have a constant stick up my ass like them.

"Dad," I said, frustrated, "I am on the right track."

What had happened at the junkyard was a complete accident, and as hot as Axl was, I was putting him out of my mind. But my parents, of course, were so worried that their prize daughter was going to shack up with a leather-clad stranger and compromise their vicarious dreams.

And honestly, the more they bitched to me, the more appealing that sounded.

"Dad," I repeated. "Axl's a nice guy who helped me out. I'll pay for the car to be towed back from the junkyard and that'll be the end of it. You won't see him again. I won't see him. I swear."

My dad looked at me, and the expression on his face betrayed his doubt. I ignored it, scooting my chair away from the table. I gave my dad and my mom each a kiss on the cheek. The talk had diminished my appetite again, so I only got an apple before heading back upstairs to my room.

I sat at my desk, opened my laptop, and pulled up my school email. Behind me, draped over the back of the chair, I felt Axl's sweatshirt. I grabbed it and chucked it in the trashcan. Fuck him, and fuck whatever he did or didn't think about me. It didn't affect me at all.

It was time to get back to work, to catch up with what I'd missed over the last two days. And it was time to completely forget about Axl Archer.

CHAPTER 11: AXL

I woke up the next morning in a cold puddle of sweat. My head pounded with an agonizing hangover, and it felt like a thousand screws were twisting into my skull. In other words, a usual morning.

After the Reaper visit last night, I'd hit the bar and downed half a bottle of Jack. Ryker sat next to me at the bar, sipping a whiskey and water, eying me with concern as I put away shot after shot. I was fucking pissed off, and hammered out of my mind when I'd decided it was time to leap on my hog to get Holly. But Ryker stopped me. "We figure this out tomorrow," he'd said, "Reapers ain't gonna find her at her parents' place tonight. Can't risk a rumble in town. And never fucking ride wasted."

The idea of her out there, alone and exposed fuckin' enraged me. But he was right. Holly was safer where she was. I hated that I felt so damn protective of her. It was dangerous.

I'd stumbled back upstairs to my room, glass in hand. There was no sign of the slut I'd bedded earlier, but I didn't give a fuck. I passed out cold.

51

And now I was paying for it. But thank fuck I hadn't spilled the drink, 'cause I needed it now. I reached over to the dresser, grabbed the glass of now-warm whiskey, and put it down the hatch.

Hair of the dog. That was a bad damn habit to get into, but I had to function today.

The fog in my brain began to lift. I forced myself out of bed and forced myself to endure a cold shower until I'd regained full control of my senses. Then I got dressed and thundered downstairs, beelining for Ryker's office, pounding my fist on the door.

"Yeah?" Ryker barked from behind the door. I swung the door open and entered, the adrenaline of last night flooding back into my body. Ryker sat in his leather chair behind his desk, and Dash and Lynch sat in guest chairs opposite to him.

Dash hanging around Lynch? What the fuck? I didn't like that.

I stormed into the room, shutting the door hard behind me.

"Nice of you to join, VP," said Ryker coolly. "How's the head treating you?"

I ignored his jab and cut to the chase.

"We can't let an innocent die," I said. "It ain't the Sons way. We protect the girl."

Ryker spoke calmly, but his words infuriated me. "VP. Been talkin' about this, and I need you to understand me now. We did what we could for this girl. We did her right, the way Sons do. But she ain't our problem now. We gotta pull in tight right now, keep brothers close and keep outsiders out. Reapers are testing us, provoking us. We can't overextend. Our cash flow's runnin' out, and shit's

52

heating up, son. Reapers even got away with most of our guns back at the junkyard. We've gotta be pragmatic."

"That's fucking bullshit," I growled. "Sons code has always said no innocents die. No ifs or buts."

Lynch glared at me, his beady eyes focused on me like lasers. He didn't break eye contact. "You got a hard-on for this bitch, and you're waving your cock in our faces. You wanna put your neck on the line for her? Then patch outta the club."

Inside, my blood boiled, my body a steamworks. I was fucking sick of Lynch challenging me and jockeying for my position. "Fuck you, Lynch," I growled.

He stood up hard, knocking his chair down behind him. He puffed out his chest, stepping toward me aggressively. I looked down at his ugly fucking mug, having at least 6 inches on him. This was the last fucking straw.

With my left hand, I reached out and grabbed his cut. My right hand drew back like a catapult, then bored straight into his face. He fell backwards on his ass, crashing onto the chair beneath him. Blood poured from his mouth. I lunged forward, raising my fist again, but Ryker and Dash had already leapt into action. Dash grabbed my fist from behind, and Ryker hopped over his desk in his catlike manner, creating a barrier between me and Lynch. If I wanted to finish off Lynch, I'd have to go through Ryker, and I wasn't prepared to do that.

The way that Ryker and Dash reacted told me that the power dynamics of the club were subtly shifting, and this troubled me. I was overplaying my hand. I'd been Ryker's favorite ever since he patched me in eight years ago, but he fuckin' owed Lynch now 'cause Lynch had taken a bullet for him a year back. Ryker never would've stepped between us before then... And now Dash was hanging around Lynch too? Something was afoot. I had to be fucking careful.

"Axl, my boy," said Ryker, putting his hands firmly on my shoulders, "get a hold of yourself." He steadied my arms.

On the ground, Lynch snarled and wiped blood on his sleeve. Dash released my fists from his grip, and stepped around me to extend a hand to Lynch, helping him up. I glared at Dash, and it pissed me the fuck off that my best buddy in the club was helping that piece of shit Lynch off the floor.

Was I on the outside now?

Ryker guided me across the room, pushing me down firmly into the chair that Dash had been in. He then leaned back against his desk. Next to us, Lynch had stood up. Dash was standing next to him.

Ryker looked at me hard. "Clear your head," he said sharply. "You've been my right hand ever since I took you off the streets, and this ain't like you. This girl, she ain't your old lady."

Next to me Dash spoke softly and deliberately. "You know he's right, buddy," he said. "She isn't our problem anymore."

"The club VP," said Ryker, "must always think clearly. And right now, you ain't."

"You're goddamn right about that," said Lynch, rubbing his jaw.

I glared at him.

"Listen, boy," said Ryker. "I know you. You were a kid on the streets when I found you. Not even 18. With nothing, no one. Just another kid in that meat grinder they call the foster system. You were alone, and that affected you. You've always stood up for those who can't protect themselves, and I admire that. But the club comes first. Always. Don't forget that."

I fumed silently. Internally, I tried to resolve to let her go, fighting a mental battle as I stood there. But my conscience fought me at every step. I couldn't fucking accept leaving Holly unprotected, ripe for the Reapers' picking.

Ryker crossed his arms and straightened his head. "Clear your head," he said again. "Take a couple days off. Go for a long ride. I don't give a shit, as long as your head is screwed on straight when you get back here. Shit's volatile right now between us and the Reapers, and we need everybody on point."

I gritted my teeth, suppressing the urge to go crazy.

"Understand?" he said.

I paused, for what seemed like forever, unable to speak. Finally, I summoned all my strength.

"Right."

"Good. Now get the hell out of here," he said.

Lynch was staring right at me, his expression signaling his seething disdain for me. Now I had enemies inside and outside the club. Lynch wanted VP, and he was unpredictable. With all the shit going down, there was no way to know what he might pull. I had to watch my back.

I about-faced and exited the room without a word, but as I stepped out into the main clubhouse, I heard Dash's voice behind me.

"Axl," he said, pulling me aside. "What the hell's gotten into you?"

Dash had been with me through thick and thin since the beginning. He was always the guy I could go to, the guy I could trust. But we were coming down on opposite sides of this issue.

"Not a goddamn thing," I grunted.

Just that I'm supposed to sit here and twiddle my fucking thumbs while the Reapers do God-knows-what to the only chick that's ever made me feel something.

I turned and walked away without saying another word.

CHAPTER 12: HOLLY

I stared into my laptop screen, squinting. I'd been working in my room since the talk with my parents, and my eyes were all red and puffy. I was trying to catch up on all the classwork I'd missed in the last two days. I hated getting behind and tried to avoid it at all costs. Playing catch-up always made things a thousand times harder.

There was barely a month and a half left until graduation, and it was going to be a pain in the ass to finish my documentary without my camera. I was going to have to borrow equipment from the school. And their cameras were all old crap that were guaranteed to slow me way down. Not to mention I had to rethink the entire project without the junkyard angle. No way was I going back there a second time.

I sighed. I minimized the web browser and opened Skype. My best friend Brooke was online.

"hey," I wrote to her, "you ever feel like your life is just a constant parade of the most ridiculous shit happening?"

"haha," she wrote back, "everyday. our lives are ridiculous. keep your head up, girl... you gonna go out with nathan this week?"

Nathan was a kid I met in my chemistry lab. He'd asked me out last week and I'd given him a tentative "yes," but I wasn't excited about it. Nice kid, I guess, but going out with him after meeting Axl was like going from a diet of French chocolate truffles to Fruit Roll-Ups. A kiddie downgrade. From man to boy. I was actually kind of afraid that Axl had spoiled my appetite for guys completely. I didn't think I was going to find another man like him at my college. Or anywhere else.

"idk," I wrote. "He's kinda lame. whatever. I'm wiped out, going to sleep. ttyl."

I sighed and shut the laptop. Bleary-eyed, I looked at the alarm clock on my nightstand. It was already eleven-'o-clock, and I only had Sunday left to finish my work before going back to class on Monday. Yep, I was going to be working all weekend. It seemed strange to be going back to everyday, mundane life after the craziness that had happened this week. But I had made myself a promise that I intended to keep. No more Axl Archer. Not even any thinking about Axl Archer. It couldn't lead anywhere good.

I got up and stumbled out of my bedroom, my feet padding quietly on the soft plush carpet of the upstairs. I crossed the hall and flicked on the light switch in the bathroom. I studied my face in the mirror. God. I was looking rough. I guessed that was what 48 hours of near-constant adrenaline and sleep deprivation did to a girl.

Sighing, I turned on the faucet and started brushing my teeth. I was still brushing when I swore I heard a sound coming from down the hall. I took the toothbrush out of my mouth, toothpaste bubbles foaming at my lips.

"Mmom?" I said into the hallway. "That you?"

There was no response. Normally I would've shrugged it off, but something felt off.

I put down the toothbrush and spit out the foam bubbles in my mouth before walking back across the hallway and peeking into my bedroom.

Nothing.

I entered my bedroom, and everything was as I'd left it. There was a cool draft coming in from the window, though, which was cracked. That was strange—I didn't make a habit of keeping my window open and I couldn't even remember the last time I'd opened it. There hadn't been a draft when I'd been sitting there working on my laptop... had there? I was so tired I couldn't be sure. But nothing else looked out of place. I probably just needed some sleep. I pushed the window closed tightly until the weather stripping sealed out the wind, and latched it again.

I went back to the bathroom, finished brushing, and then returned to my bedroom. I shut the door with a click and turned the lights off. My eyes relaxed, adjusting to the dark. Only a faint moon glow came in through the window.

For the first time in nearly three days, I was finally alone—actually alone, with no one watching me or bothering me. It was an incredible relief.

I padded along the carpet, and flopped down onto my bed, pulling the covers over me. The soft pillows cradled my head and it felt so good to finally be in my own bed again. If only I didn't have to wake up to an alarm clock the next morning. I felt like I could sleep for days.

In spite of myself, my mind began to wander back to the events of the weekend as I drifted off to sleep. As hard as I tried, I couldn't flush the thought of Axl out of my head. Couldn't forget his incredibly handsome face, his smell, his touch, his taste. I replayed the memory of our roadside encounter in my head, and felt wet between my legs. My hand began to find its way down my stomach, and my fingers slipped under the elastic waistband of my panties. I closed my eyes.

And then a gloved hand covered my mouth. I opened my eyes and screamed instinctively, but my scream was completely stifled as if someone had hit my mute button. An intruder wearing a black coat and ski mask stood over me, his hand pressing hard against my mouth. A second, shorter masked figure stood by my closet.

Fuck—the closet! I instantly knew what had happened—they'd come in through the window and were waiting in my closet the entire time I was brushing my teeth. A sick feeling flooded my stomach. I'd always felt safe in my own house, but now it was clear that feeling was only an illusion.

I wished Axl were here.

I wiggled, struggling to free my mouth from under the man's glove, but he only pressed harder. And then, with his other hand, he reached behind his back and pulled out a gun.

CHAPTER 13: AXL

I paced back and forth in my room, Ryker's orders ringing in my ears. Orders to let Holly go, to let the Reapers exact their vengeance on her.

And for what? Yeah, she'd seen shit, but she wasn't a part of it. That was what separated the Sons from pieces of shit like the Reapers. A little fucking common decency and a code of ethics.

"Goddammit!" I shouted, and drove my fist into the wall. My knuckles seared in pain, and a hairline crack flicked through the wooden wall.

I couldn't get her face out of my head. Her smile, her smell, the way she tucked her hair over her ears. Those big, brown, honest eyes.

Fuck it. I was going to get that girl, even if it meant going against my own club. Consequences be damned. Ryker could be made to understand.

Maybe.

I grabbed my cut from the back of my chair and threw it on. Then I grabbed my gunbelt, lashed it around my waist, and pulled out my desk drawer. My black polymer

Glock lay in the drawer, atop a stack of cash and magazines. I grabbed the Glock and a loaded mag and shoved it inside. I chambered a round and jammed the Glock into the holster on my belt.

I exited the room and crashed down the stairs into the main clubhouse. It was eerily quiet tonight. Most guys had gone home to their families for a few days, laying low and preparing for shit with the Reapers. There was only the bartender and two guys drinking—my buddy Dash and a new prospect.

Dash looked up as I came down the stairs.

He knew.

"VP, buddy," he said, bouncing up from his barstool. The prospect and bartender watched quietly. "Lemme talk to you real quick."

"No time," I said flatly, heading for the main exit. But Dash sped up to intercept me and pulled me aside before I reached the door.

"Buddy," he said, lowering his voice to a whisper, his expression a cross between concern and suspicion, "Don't do this, man. You're thinking with your dick. This ain't you."

My posture stiffened and the veins in my neck pulsed. "This ain't some whore who had it coming. She's an innocent. Can't let the Reapers do this to her."

Dash exhaled slowly, tension boiling beneath the surface. "Then you ain't my VP right now, brother."

"And if we're gonna toss an innocent girl to the Reapers, then this ain't my club," I said. "Now get the fuck outta my way."

Dash looked at me silently, the moment seeming to stretch infinitely in time. Finally, he looked down and stepped aside. I left the clubhouse, hopped on my bike, and raged through the city streets.

As I ran stop signs and cut corners, my bike blazing over the city blocks and shattering the quiet Saturday night of Coppertail, my heart pounded in my chest. If they'd gotten to her first...

When I finally pulled onto her street, I saw an unmarked van parked on the street opposite to her house. A van like that didn't belong in Coppertail.

"Fuck!" I yelled, pounding my fist against the handlebars. I locked the bike's front and back brakes with my right hand and foot, the bike's rear wheel squealing and fishtailing as I skidded to a stop, nearly going off the road into a ditch.

I swung the kickstand out hard, and leapt off my bike. I ran toward the house, adrenaline pumping through my veins. Finally, for the first time in days, the perpetual hangover feeling in my head lifted completely. I felt fucking alive and ready for action. This was Axl fucking Archer in his natural state.

I bounded up the steps to the front door of the house and tried the handle. Locked. The front door was undisturbed. If they'd already busted in, they'd done it a different way.

I raced back down the stairs and around the side of the house—and that's when I heard the ruckus coming from an upstairs bedroom.

Shit. They were inside and they'd gotten to her first.

My brain and body finally firing on all cylinders, I urgently scanned the side of the house and willed a solution to come to me. And it did, like I knew it would. I thrived under pressure.

The tree. I scrambled up the branches, hoisting my weight up from limb to limb until I came face-to-face with the upstairs window. The scene I saw inside fucking enraged me, setting every fiber of my being on fire. Holly was sitting on the edge of her bed, her hands bound behind her back, a cloth gag stuffed in her mouth. Two men stood over her, one of them typing into the glowing screen of a cell phone.

I'd been in this lifestyle long enough to know that her being bound and gagged was a good thing. If these two fucks aimed to hurt her, they would've done it already. They wanted her alive, and that gave me the opening I needed.

I dropped down from the tree, not taking the time to descend the way I'd come up. My ankles and knees seared in pain as they absorbed the impact of my fall, but I gritted my teeth and ignored the pain. I sprinted back across the street where I'd parked my bike. I grabbed the handlebars and kicked out with my foot to retract the kickstand. Then, I shoved my bike backwards, letting it fall out of sight into the ditch behind the road. Normally I'd go fucking livid at the thought of my bike dropping, but with Holly's life on the line, I didn't need to think twice. My bike tipped over with a crash, out of sight.

I darted over to the van, crouching down on the side facing away from Holly's house. I reached into my boot and pulled my knife out of its sheath—I couldn't fire my damn Glock on a quiet night in a neighborhood full of families.

I gripped my knife hard, and I waited. Tonight was lights out for those Reaper fucks.

CHAPTER 14: HOLLY

My heart pounded as I sat on the edge of my bed with my hands tied and my mouth gagged. I'd fought them as hard as I could. I'd gotten out from under the tall one's grip, and bitten his hand until I felt the tendons crunch between my teeth. I'd turned my head afterward, preparing for a retaliatory blow to my head, but it hadn't come.

The reply, which came through gritted teeth, was worse: "Fucking try that again, and we go find everyone else in this house."

I was scared to death, but no matter what happened to me, I wasn't going to let my parents get involved in this. No matter how angry they made me sometimes, they didn't deserve this. So I shut my mouth and let them tie me up.

After I was bound, the one whose hand I bit pulled out his phone, his palm wrapped in a white t-shirt from my dresser. He tapped on it for a few seconds and then waited. Neither man spoke until the phone buzzed in reply a minute later. He read the message on the phone and then said, "Anyone else awake in this house?"

I shook my head no.

"I hope for their sake you're tellin' the truth. We're going downstairs. Walk."

I had no choice but to lead the men through my house, past my parents' closed bedroom door, and down the stairs. As we walked, I held my breath, tiptoeing as gently as possible.

The tall one with the bitten hand led the way, while the shorter, fatter one followed behind me, his hand on the rope lashed around my wrists. When we got to the front door, the tall one opened it, and led me out of my house into the cold, dark night.

I was terrified of what might happen to me, but at the same time I was beyond relieved that we'd gotten out of the house without my parents waking up. I couldn't bear to think what could've happened if they'd woken up.

The men rushed me across the street toward a black van with painted-over windows, which was parallel parked on the side of the street opposite my house. They led me around to the rear of the van, and the tall one opened the door.

That's when Axl flew around the side of the van. His body sprung into action like an angry animal, a murderous expression on his face. In his hand I saw the streetlight reflecting off a shining blade. The tall one never saw it coming when Axl raised his arm above his head and brought the blade plunging down into the side of the man's neck.

I screamed under my gag, struggling to pull away from the short man behind me. I twisted my body, wrenching my bound hands out of his grip. As I did so, I met Axl's eyes as he yanked the knife out of the tall man's neck. Blood spurted out like a fountain, splashing over Axl's chest and face.

As my hands came free from the man's grip, I threw my body toward the ditch on the side of the road. As a young girl, I used to sit in the ditch and have picnics with my grandma. But this time I crashed headfirst into a huge block of metal as I fell, disorienting me. I realized it was a motorcycle as I lay dazed, coughing. I could see Axl holding the knife and the short man fumbling in his jacket for his gun.

The man never had a chance—Axl was too fast. His arm flew backwards like a piston, and then drilled forward, the knife plunging through the short man's jacket and straight into his chest. He let out an agonizing scream that melted into a bloody gurgle as the knife carved up his lungs inside his chest. Still laying on my back in the ditch, I looked on, horrified. The short man collapsed to the ground as his gurgling scream died out and his life left his body.

Axl left his knife in the man's chest as he raced over to where I lay in the ditch.

"Holly!" he said, his voice dark and husky in the night. "You hurt?"

I shook my head no. Axl reached down and pulled the gag out of my mouth.

"Axl, what the fuck," I said. I was now officially beyond freaked-the-fuck out. This was way more than I bargained for.

"Holly," he said, turning me on my side to untie the rope around my hands, "I'm fuckin' sorry. Those Reapers— they're filthy fucking animals."

As I lay in the ditch, everything felt so intense, so visceral. I was wide awake, and all my senses were working in overdrive. Finally Axl succeeded in freeing my hands. I reached up and he grabbed my hands with his, pulling me to my feet. He rubbed the skin of my wrists, which were raw and red.

"Holly," he said, looking into my eyes, "We've gotta get the hell out of here." He wrapped his hands around me, pulling me closer. I shivered, not realizing how cold I'd been. His embrace made me feel completely safe and protected, just like back in the pickup truck. It was magic— I didn't think anything could comfort me right now, but he did.

I nodded, blinking hard, trying to think straight. "I can go to my friend Brooke's house," I said.

"No. Fuck that," said Axl. "You're comin' with me until this blows over."

Oh my god, I thought. Not again. I felt my dream of competing at the indie film festivals slipping away from me. And graduation—I couldn't afford to miss any more classes. But what fucking choice did I have?

"What about my parents?"

Axl's forehead wrinkled, his eyes squeezed closed in thought.

"You gotta tell 'em to get outta here. They can go to the cops if they need to."

A lump formed in my throat.

"Fuck," I whispered. I looked at the two men lying on the ground next to their van. "What happens when the cops find them?"

"That ain't happening. Somebody's gonna come clean this shit up stat," Axl said, grimacing. "I'm gonna stash these guys in the back of their van for now."

"What about the blood?"

He grimaced again. "It'll be gone before dawn. Right now you gotta get your stuff and leave a note for your parents. Tell 'em to bounce."

I swallowed hard. "Okay."

I hurried back toward my house. As I started across the street, out of the corner of my eye I saw Axl dragging the men's bodies into the back of their van.

CHAPTER 15: AXL

While Holly grabbed her stuff, I crammed the two dirty Reaper carcasses into the back of the van. I thanked fuck that this had gone down in boring-ass Coppertail; not a soul drove past while I loaded up the van. And no one noticed that when I backed it up ten feet, it was to cover the massive pool of blood on the asphalt.

I put the van in park, pulled out my cell phone, and sent a text to the contact in my book named "Mr. Clean." The Sons contracted him to take care of fucked-up situations like this. I grimaced at the thought of the drain this'd be on my bank account—this was a personal call, not a club call, and a nighttime rush job at that. Mr. Clean didn't work cheap.

I exited the van and slammed the door, locking the keys inside as Holly came out of her house. As long as he got here before the Reapers did, we'd have a head start. Mr. Clean would be doing a good deed, I thought wryly. By getting the carcasses outta here, he'd be saving the neighborhood from a god-forsaken smell when the sun came up in the morning.

"I'm ready," said Holly, apprehensively. She had a small red backpack slung around her shoulder.

I stepped off the road into the ditch, hauling my bike upright. It was too dark to see the damage, but I had no doubt it'd need some fuckin' bodywork after that. Pissed me off, but I'd done what I had to.

I pulled off my cut and surveyed it. It was splattered in Reaper blood. Now there was a badge of pride if I'd ever seen one. I grinned at my jacket, and if it'd had a mouth, it would've grinned right back. But I couldn't wear this thing right now. It'd just be another target on our backs—literally.

I stuffed the cut into a saddlebag, but not before using the clean side to wipe the fuckin' blood off my face. "Let's go," I said.

We mounted the bike, and we rode the hell away from that bloodbath.

I took us to an old hideout of mine. An old, decrepit motel in the desert near the California border where no one ever fucked with you. It was full of people who couldn't afford to fuck with you. Everyone there was running from someone.

The guy at the check-in desk was an old, stodgy-looking dude with thick-rimmed metal glasses. The lobby was small and hot despite the cool night, and it reminded me more of a gas station than a hotel lobby. The clerk sat behind thick, bulletproof glass.

"Yeah," he grunted.

"Room for two," I said. "No check-out date."

The man casually thumbed through a ledger book in front of him, a look of disinterest on his face. Then he looked up, and his gaze switched from me, to Holly, and back.

"You ain't just want an hour?" he said. "Discount rate."

"Hey," said Holly, "What the hell does that mean?"

I shook my head in disgust. This asshole was a real creepy old fucker. "She ain't a whore," I said, leaning forward and looking down my nose at the man, "She's my woman."

Out of the corner of my eye, I saw Holly shift uncomfortably, but she said nothing. The man looked at her again, shrugged, then pushed his glasses up the bridge of his nose and booked us a room.

We exited the lobby and began walking back toward the bike. The sun was starting to come up, and the distant sound of desert birds echoed across the dawn. Holly remained silent until we'd grabbed our stuff from the bike. We were walking across the motel's parking lot to our room when she spoke.

"You think I'm your 'woman?'" she said. "I barely know you and all you've done is fuck up my life. I wish I'd never gone to that junkyard."

I halted my walk, stopping short in the middle of the parking lot. Goddammit. I was sticking my neck out for this chick 'cause I thought maybe I felt something for her. And I thought she did too. Had I been thinking with my cock this whole time just like Dash said?

"I saved your ass back there," I said, angrily. "I'm your bodyguard right now. So yeah, that makes you my woman."

"Umm, I'm pretty sure it doesn't work like that," said Holly.

"So you don't *wanna* be my woman?" I asked hotly. It just came out, and I was shocked I'd said it. I wasn't the kind of guy to say stupid shit around women.

72

"You've gotta be kidding me," she said, shaking her head.

"Whatever," I replied. I turned and started back toward the motel room. Her words stayed in the back of my mind, pissing me off.

When we got inside, the interior of our motel room was dark and dingy. The decor looked like it hadn't been updated since the 70s. And to be honest... there was something about it that I really enjoyed.

Just my style.

"Hmm," I muttered under my breath. "Only one bed."

Holly frowned. "Maybe you should go back out there and ask for a roll-away."

"Maybe you should go ask," I shot back at her, annoyed. "I'm sure ol' dirty bastard back there would love to help."

"Whatever," said Holly crossly. She hung her backpack on the back of a chair and sat down on the edge of the bed, holding her head in her hands.

I went into the bathroom. It was a fuckin' pigsty, just like every other time I'd been by this joint. I turned the sink on hot enough to burn, and scrubbed my hands and face 'til they were nearly raw. Had to get all that fuckin' Reaper juice off me.

"God," Holly said as I walked out of the bathroom, rubbing my face with a towel, "I'm so fucking tired. I was gonna get my first night's sleep all week, and then everything went to hell."

"I ain't exactly been sleeping tight either, darlin'," I said. "Club wars tend to do that to me."

She ignored me and kept rubbing her temples. Then she said, "I'm gonna take a shower."

She grabbed her backpack again and disappeared into the bathroom. "This place is filthy," she said, coming back out of the bathroom.

I shrugged. "The Four Seasons was all outta rooms in the middle of fucking nowhere."

Holly shut the door hard. Jesus Christ. She was a real piece of work.

I walked to the window next to the front door and bent my knees to peek outside, holding the blinds open with my thumb and forefinger. My bike sat outside, undisturbed. I heard music coming from a room across the way—at this fucking hour, Christ—but there was no sign of trouble.

Sighing, I opened the door, stepped outside, and took in the calmness of the dawn. It was a stark contrast from the chaos that'd gone down just a couple hours ago. I really could've used a smoke, even though I'd quit years ago.

When I finally went back into the room, Holly was lying on one edge of the bed, wrapped in a crappy, threadbare towel from the motel. Her arms were crossed over her chest, hugging her breasts tight against her body.

God, under any other circumstances I would've been lusting over that tight young body. But right now I was just cashed the fuck out.

I crashed down on the opposite edge of the bed I stared at the ceiling for a while, processing what had just happened, not speaking. She didn't speak either.

When I finally looked over at her, a tear was running down her cheek.

I reached my hand out across the bed and nudged her arm. "Hey," I said, "Everything's gonna be cool."

"It's not," she said with a sniffle. "Graduation was only a few weeks out. Now we're in the middle of this shit. I don't know if I'll ever get to go home again."

"Darlin'," I said, covering her hand with mine, "This shit'll blow over. It always does. They'll forget all about you when the next big thing comes up. Until then, I'll protect you."

"Why?" she asked. "Doesn't your club need you right now?"

I sighed. "I disobeyed orders when I came for you."

She turned her head to look at me, her eyes watery and wide. "Why would you do that?"

I struggled for words. I wasn't used to this emotional bullshit.

"You... made me feel..." I stopped. What a fuckin' pussy I was being. "I just didn't wanna see you get fucked up," I finished.

Sometimes I fuckin' amazed myself with my own eloquence.

There was a pause, and then I felt her moving her hand in mine. She linked her fingers with my fingers and squeezed my hand. Suddenly, I couldn't resist her anymore. I turned on my side, leaned toward her, and placed my lips on hers.

She kissed me back.

CHAPTER 16: HOLLY

Axl kissed me, and I kissed him. He cupped my cheek in the palm of his calloused hand, his weathered, dry skin scratching my freshly moisturized face. The same hand that had plunged a knife into the neck of one Reaper and into the gut of another, now held my face tenderly. The contrast floated at the top of my mind while his lips mashed against mine. His breath was hot with adrenaline, a masculine, animal scent that penetrated me completely.

I loved it.

I darted my tongue out and it clashed with his, our flesh dancing and circling in lust.

"Babe," he said, pulling away for a breath, "I want you."

An excited streak of sexual possibility ran up my spine. Goosebumps tingled over my skin. His face was so handsome even in the dim motel light. His high cheekbones framed his strong, flat chin, covered in a beard as black as his full head of rich, dark hair.

This was just one more step toward madness, a further descent into the life of chaos that I seemed to be plunging toward at an alarming rate. But I was already in this deep, and every bundle of nerves in my body fired in response to his touch. God, I needed him.

Still facing him and laying on my side, I reached out to reciprocate his touch. His prickly face scratched my hands, just as his hands had. Every part of him was sharp and dangerous, a testament to the lifestyle he lived.

As I felt his face, the cheap motel towel fell away from my body, revealing my soft, perky breasts to him for the first time.

"Darlin'," he said, running his hand down my side, pulling the towel further down, "You are fuckin' perfect."

He pushed me onto my back and straddled me. My nipples were hard like pink pencil erasers. They pointed upward at him, seeking his touch, his pinch, his lips.

He dipped his head down, taking one nipple into his mouth and sucking it. My body instantly responded. I felt myself getting slick, my pussy aching, revealing my fundamental biological yearning for his body.

Axl's t-shirt hugged his torso tightly, his muscular chest and shoulders straining against the cotton, pushing the fabric to its limits. Laying on my back, I reached up, my hands exploring the ridges between his abs, taking in the flat hardness of his stomach, the sheer size and thickness of his forearms. Every touch heightened my arousal, increasing my need and hunger for him.

My towel was now completely off, cast aside on the bed, my full nakedness on display to him as he sat atop me, eclipsing me with his strong frame and pressing me into the sheets. He crouched back, the jeans on his ass pressing against my knees. He pressed his palm hard into my hip, his thumbs following the folds of my skin down to my dripping pussy. He pressed a thumb onto my swollen clit, sending waves of pleasure up my spine.

"God, babe, I'm gonna fucking stretch you out. This pussy is mine."

He scooted back again, dipping his head down against my lower belly. His tongue tickled my skin as he tasted my freshly-washed skin. His lips and mouth moved further down, below my naked waist, and settled against my pussy lips. I shuddered in pleasure as his tongue flicked and circled my clit. Axl ate my pussy ferociously, his lips chaotically spreading my slickness over my thighs and ass.

"God," he said, pausing, "you taste fucking delicious." Then he commanded, in a tone so authoritative that I couldn't resist, "On all fours. Now."

I obeyed, flipping over. I pressed my ass into the air toward him, my back arching, my muscles instinctively moving to welcome him inside me.

I looked over my shoulder. He pulled his t-shirt over his head, revealing the gorgeous body underneath, sculpted by years on the streets. He unbuckled his jeans, throwing the belt on the ground. He reached into his jeans and pulled out his hard cock. He was fully erect, his hardness throbbing. It must've been eight inches. And it was thick.

He pressed its tip against my pussy lips, and slid it in hard. An instant feeling of fullness overtook me, my muscles clenching against him. I cried out as he penetrated me, and the shock of his size left me feeling torn open. But the feeling of pain quickly gave way to pleasure as he thrust out... and in, and out.

"How'd this fucking pussy get so tight," he said, his voice husky. His hands squeezed my ass hard. I was utterly exposed, completely open to him, and my need for him only increased with every stroke.

"Oh, fuck me harder," I said, my voice a whisper amid the intense pleasure inside me.

I felt a powerful hand on my back, then a forearm. He pressed down onto my back, forcing it hard into the mattress, arching my back even further, positioning me to take his hard cock even deeper inside. The mattress muffled my cries of pleasure, and I wiggled my ass against him, grinding into his hips, wanting to feel every brush of his balls against my clit.

He held me down tight, and I couldn't have broken free even if I'd wanted to. My most private parts were utterly exposed to him. In spite of my best judgment, I was like a bitch in heat for him.

I twisted my head, doing my best to come up for air and speak. I inhaled and it felt like my body shunted the fresh breath of oxygen straight into my pussy. I felt like I was on fire.

"Fill me up," I moaned.

"Yeah," he said, breathing heavily, his voice gravelly. "I'm gonna shoot this hot cum so deep inside you."

"Oh, do it," I said with a moan. "Do it, baby."

I squeezed as hard as I could, tightening my muscles around his cock, my pussy lips stretching to their maximum to accommodate his girth. That must've sent him over the edge, because I felt a pulsing inside me, and a hot flooding feeling inside me. It brought my own orgasm to the surface like nothing else could.

"Oh, god," I said, "I'm gonna cum." My pussy began to contract, and I saw stars as I squeezed my eyes shut hard, my pussy exploding and milking every drop of biker cum out of his balls.

His thrusting slowed, and I collapsed onto my belly, spent, his cock sliding out of me. He dropped to the bed next to me, and put an arm around me, holding me tight.

We began to drift off to sleep together there, his hot seed dripping out of me and fulfilling me so totally.

CHAPTER 17: AXL

My head buzzed with dopamine and my cock was still hard despite the massive load I'd just shot into her. Jesus fuck. I'd never come like that in my life.

I watched her breasts rise and fall, her head nestled into the crook of my arm. I hadn't decided whether to let her sleep or to wake her up for round two. My balls were already replenishing their store, and right now there was nothing that could satisfy me—except a whole night of orgasms deep inside that tight pussy of hers.

Christ. Was I going crazy? Was I *really* disobeying direct fucking orders just to get my dick wet in this girl? Or was there truly something else, some deeper connection?

My thoughts drifted into dreams, becoming wilder and more surreal, until I slipped completely into the dream world.

Holly and I slept, our bodies exhausted in more ways than one, finally recuperating from the chaos of the last several days.

Around eight in the morning, our sleep was interrupted by my cell phone ringing. My eyes blasted open. Waking up fast was a talent that I'd been forced to cultivate.

God fucking dammit. Couldn't get any fucking peace and quiet. Ever.

Holly's eyes fluttered open as I reached over her to grab my phone from the nightstand.

"Yeah?"

It was Dash.

"VP. Been calling you for an hour."

"Spotty service here."

"I know," said Dash. "Calling you 'cause the Reapers are onto you, man. Lynch just clashed with one of their crews down in Rosita. Put the squeeze on one of their guys and said you're being tracked. They got to the van before Clean could take care of it."

"Fuck," I said. I hadn't expected them to react so quickly. "We'll move." Then I added, "And Ryker?"

There was a long pause on the other end of the line. "What do you think, VP? There's gonna be hell to pay."

"Had to do this, man," I said. "Can't let an innocent die." I looked over at Holly and saw her listening alertly. "Ain't the Sons way."

But the truth was, under the surface I was questioning my motives just as much as Dash was. Was I fucking lying to myself about the reason I was here? Was I really doing this out of loyalty to the Sons charter, or was I seeing things sideways because I was falling—

No. No, this was about holding the club to a higher standard than those fucking Reapers. I'd have done the same for any innocent. Maybe without the fucking, though. Yeah, that's what I told myself.

"Look man, I owe you when this all blows over. I'm heading up to Four Corners, further out of Reaper territory. Keep shit together in town. Be careful. Shit's moving fast right now."

"Yeah, boss," said Dash. There was a hell of a lot of doubt in his voice, and I knew why. If I couldn't make the guys come around to my side of this when I got back, I was facing a vote of no confidence as VP. And meanwhile the club was going into a rapidly heating war without me.

I hit the End key on the phone hard and slammed it onto the nightstand.

Holly's eyes were wide. "What was that all about?"

"Reapers found the van on your street. They want my head now. And yours."

"Damn," she said, but her voice didn't waver. I was fucking impressed with how well she was maintaining her composure. Maybe she was starting to get used to this shit. She was pretty fucking tough, not just for a college girl, but for anyone. Hell, I'd known some prospects in my time that didn't have the balls she did.

"Yeah," I said. "Get your stuff. We're going."

We forced ourselves out of bed and Holly hurriedly repacked her backpack. Christ, at least she'd had a change of clothes. I was still wearing the same shit I'd worn when I shanked those fucking Reapers, and I felt absolutely filthy.

My wish to get clean came true in an unexpected way. As we thundered down state highways, rushing toward the northern border, the skies darkened with an early morning monsoon. There was thunder, lightning, and then finally rain. I normally fucking hated rain on a ride, especially how it stung my skin at highway speeds. But as sheets of water crashed down over us, I welcomed every drop. It washed away my blood, sweat, cum, and sin.

We got to Four Corners around noon, where Arizona met New Mexico, Colorado, and Utah. We'd ridden out of the storm, and we were nearly dry by the time we arrived. Last night followed by the natural shower this morning had left me feeling more refreshed than I'd been in a while. My head was clear, my wits and senses were about me, and for once my body wasn't working overtime to clear a hangover out of my system.

I parked the bike in the visitor parking center of the Four Corners plaza, a big wide open area with a few buildings around the perimeter, and the four-way border right in the middle. Tourists milled about, and the day was shaping up to be sunny but cool. I'd become so used to living life in the dark, hard clubhouse, and in bars and warehouses that it was a fucking shock to be outside like this. And to be up and about by noon in the first place. Shit, maybe this Reaper situation wasn't so fucking bad after all, I thought to myself. These fuckers were upping my productivity like nobody's business. I chuckled out loud.

"I'm fucking starving," I said. "Let's grab some food."

We found a food truck serving Navajo food, and I ordered some fry bread and beans for the both of us.

Holly and I sat down at a bench. She pressed her leg against mine, and my cock stiffened in my pants as I replayed the events of last night in my head. I was gonna fuck her silly the next time we got a little peace and quiet.

But right now we sat together like some fucking couple or something, having a picnic at the park in the middle of the day. What a fucking ridiculous way for Axl Archer to spend a morning.

I needed to get my shit together.

CHAPTER 18: HOLLY

Axl and I sat on the bench in silence, munching on Navajo fry bread and beans, soaking up the sun's rays. The bread was so greasy, but it was exactly what I needed. I'd hardly eaten anything in the last few days and my body was starving for calories.

I thought about last night, how badly I'd wanted Axl and how utterly fulfilling it was when he'd finally taken me while I kneeled in total submission. I'd never wanted it from anyone the way I wanted it from him. I loved the way he took control, loved the way it felt to be his fuck toy. I hated to admit it to myself, but I thought I was actually starting to feel something for him. Something real. I mean, he'd been there for me in my time of need. Who else had put their life on the line for me?

I wondered if he felt the same way about me, or if I was just another cum hole for him. Maybe he just felt fucking sorry for me and thought he'd help me avoid becoming a stain on McClellan Street like those two guys. I mean, even dogs don't deserve to die like that. And if he met someone more beautiful, with bigger tits, with a better ass, who knows what would happen to this.

Whatever "this" was.

I was still hungry after we'd demolished the pile of beans. "I'm gonna go get seconds," I said.

"Damn," said Axl, and let out a loud belch. "How are you still hungry?"

I wrinkled my nose. "You're a pig."

I returned to the food truck and ordered more of what we'd gotten before. When I turned around to walk back, Axl was watching a kid struggle to fly a kite. I watched from a distance, him facing away from me. But just as I started to walk back to the bench, Axl stood up and walked over to the kid.

He crouched down, taking himself down to kid height. He helped the boy wind the string the right way and ran alongside him, showing him how to get the kite to catch the wind. With Axl's help, the red kite surged into the air, climbing the breeze, going higher and higher.

That was about the last thing I'd expected to see from Axl Archer.

When the kid had finally gotten the kite in the air, I saw a woman rushing toward the child. She bent down and picked him up, her eyes turning toward Axl suspiciously. I saw them linger—probably unable to look away from his handsome face even while regarding his rough, tattooed appearance with suspicion.

He turned around and caught me watching as I nibbled on a piece of fry bread. He walked toward me.

"Wow," I said, "Since when do big bad bikers fly kites with little kids?"

He grunted, and it seemed like he was concealing something beneath the surface. "Little kids, you know, they just haven't seen shit. Haven't had the world shit on them yet."

I ate slowly, pondering his words. "What about you? I asked, trying to imagine Axl as a kid. "When did life take its shit on you?"

A fleeting grimace flashed over his face. "It's always been that way for me," he said. "I never knew my real parents." He added, "Foster system, you know."

I instantly felt guilty for asking. "Damn. That sucks."

"Yeah, well, guess that's how you end up like me," he said.

"Like what?"

"Like a fucking scumbag who people don't want their kids to be around."

I chewed in thought, saying nothing. We began to walk in silence, heading toward the point where the four states met.

Finally he spoke. "Yeah. You wouldn't understand. Pretty college girl with two parents." He laughed and there was a tone of cruelty in his laugh.

"No, *you* don't understand," I shot back, heat rising in my stomach. Anger and resentment that had been brewing under the surface were starting to come out. "You should walk a fucking block in my shoes right now. My parents are always up my ass about everything. And now four years of work down the drain. I'm gonna get dropped from my classes 'cause of this. Unlike you, I actually have a future. Well, had a future."

"Oh, fuck off," he said angrily. "Real fucking hard to repeat a semester while I save you ass. You're living a real hard life."

I stopped walking and turned angrily to face him, my face beet red. "You know, my parents probably think you killed those guys on the street. Which you did. And they're probably sitting around the police station right now, wondering where the hell they went wrong with me. Wondering when and if they're going to be able to go home again. Honestly, this life of yours, with the motorcycles and the club, it's a total piece of shit. You can't just fucking kill people left and right and solve all your problems with violence. You're a bunch of fucking animals."

Axl's eyes narrowed, his jaw muscles tensing and a look of anger flashed across his face. "You don't choose this life," he said, "It chooses you. It chose me a long time ago. And it chose you when you got involved in our business. Without me, you'd be fucking dead already. Things have changed for you darlin'. You're in this deep and the sooner you come to terms with that, the better."

I was angry. Angry at how he talked to me. Angry that I'd given myself up to him last night. Axl Archer and I were about as different as two people could be. Stupid me for thinking that something good might come out of this whole mess. Stupid me for thinking just a few hours ago that I might be falling for him. He was a real asshole.

Then, a loud bang split my ears, and Axl stumbled. A stream of bright red blood flowed down his arm.

CHAPTER 19: AXL

I didn't want to be cruel, but I couldn't help it. What did a chick like Holly know about fucking struggle? Was I supposed to get on my knees and grovel about spoiling her graduation plans by saving her ass from the Reapers? And now it was my fault she couldn't impress her parents with a paper diploma?

All while I risked life and limb—not to mention my future with the Sons—just to keep her safe.

This was just one of the many reasons the club lifestyle made sense to me. No bullshit diplomas, no bullshit authorities hanging over your head. Just money and mayhem.

But at the same time, no matter how much she pissed me off, no matter how much she didn't understand the new world she was in, I wouldn't be able to fucking live with myself if something happened to her.

I was opening my mouth to snap at her when I heard the gunshot. A civilian might've thought it was a car backfiring, but I'd been around enough fucking gunfights my first year in the club alone to know the difference. I knew the sound of gunfire like I knew my way around pussy.

I didn't even realize I'd been hit until I saw her eyes lock onto my shoulder in horror. She stood there, frozen, not having developed the street instincts that I had—the ones that told me to get the fuck down.

And the crazy thing is, as I pushed her to the ground behind a nearby SUV and saw the blood pouring out of my arm, my only thought was to thank God that it'd been me and not her.

The Reapers had somehow fucking found us.

"Oh my god," said Holly, clasping her hand over her mouth. "What can I do?"

I gritted my teeth in pain, crouching down behind the vehicle, trying to simultaneously cover Holly with my body and pull my Glock out of my belt holster with my uninjured arm. "Pressure," I said. My shoulder felt like it'd been hit with the claw end of a flaming hammer.

Holly pressed her palm against my shoulder, and pain seared through my chest and arm. Phantom pains fired out of the wound, triggering nerves in my neck. I clenched my teeth and fought through the pain, peeking out from behind the SUV, my eyes scanning for the shooter. Tourists were running and screaming, piling into their minivans and sedans in the parking lot. Not only did I have to protect Holly, I had to work against the clock and get us out of here alive before the place filled up with the ice.

As I peeked around the corner, another shot rang out, and I felt a shockwave traveling through the air as a bullet whizzed past my head. Fuck. That was rifle fire.

"What the hell do we do?" Holly asked in a panicked, urgent voice. "You're bleeding a lot."

"I'm going back into the plaza," I said, "Can't see a goddamn thing from here. Stay put."

I gripped my Glock hard, and dashed out from behind the safety of the SUV, sprinting back toward the bench we'd been sitting at earlier. There were more gunshots, but they echoed across the surrounding valley and it was impossible to tell where they came from.

As I ran toward the bench, I caught a glint of light off a metal object in the window of a Ford Explorer parked across the plaza. The barrel of a rifle. There was no fucking way to know if it was the only shooter. But no matter what, I'd have to take out this fuck if I had any hope of getting Holly to the bike.

I snaked my way around the perimeter of the plaza, taking cover behind trees as I rounded the circle. I was going to complete the circuit and flank the Explorer on the rear, get close enough to where I could light it up with my Glock. And if someone tried going across the plaza toward Holly, they were fucking fodder to me.

But I didn't make it all the way around. I was bleeding heavily and by the time I'd gotten three-fourths of the way to the Ford, I felt lightheaded and fell to my knees, wheezing. I tried to stand up but my legs were lead, my body low on blood.

I sat on my ass, and backed myself up against a tree. I rotated around the trunk, taking myself out of the shooter's line of sight.

Fight, I told myself. *Reapers won't show her any mercy.*

A voice called out from the other side of the tree. "Archer!"

I twisted my head and yelled around the tree trunk. "She ain't a part of this, you fucks!"

"Archer," the voice boomed, "Surrender and she lives."

"I need a guarantee," I sputtered as loudly as I could. My voice was weakening, hoarse.

"You ain't got a choice. Plaza's covered in your blood."

Fuck. I was fucked up, and I had failed. I knew these cunts all too well. They'd finish me off, then Holly, no matter what they promised.

"Fuck you," I coughed. "You want me, come get me." I pulled my knees up to my chest and held my Glock out in front of me, steadying it against my knees as best I could. If I was gonna go out, I was gonna take as many piece of shit Reapers with me as I could.

"Don't need to. You're gonna bleed out behind that tree."

Anger surged inside of me. I wanted to fucking murder this piece of shit. But I was frozen in place, unable to muster the strength to stand.

Suddenly, there was a dull thud and a gurgling moan. Then Holly came into my field of view, holding a brick dripping with blood.

"Holly," I said, my voice a gurgle.

"I couldn't just sit there," she said.

Goddamn. She had fucking saved my ass. I felt a new surge of strength inside me.

"Help me," I said, and I took her arm, hauling myself to my feet. I was dizzy, but my shoulder had finally stopped pouring blood.

Leaning against Holly, I hobbled over to the man laying on the ground, a pool of blood seeping out from under his black ski mask. I reached down and pulled it off his head. I recognized him—Mario Gutierrez, a veteran of the Demons MC. What the fuck? Sons had no beef with the Demons. Something was fucked up.

Feeling my strength come back to me, I howled into the air. I smashed my fist down onto the dead man's face over and over again, until it was a bloody stump.

CHAPTER 20: HOLLY

I stood over the man, brick in my hand, heart pounding in my chest. When I'd brought it crashing down on his head from behind with all my strength, he'd let out an anguished, garbled cry and collapsed to the ground like a sack of rocks.

There hadn't been time to think. When I'd seen Axl stumble and press himself up against the tree, I knew he was losing his strength, and that I had to do something. So I'd grabbed a loose brick from the wall I hid behind, and rushed straight across the plaza with it in hand, snuck up behind the masked intruder, and caught him by surprise.

Then I'd helped Axl up. He'd pulled off the intruder's ski mask, and I instantly knew that something was wrong. Even more wrong than it already was. Then he pounded the dead man's face into the cement. I was aghast at the display of violence and brutality. I'd never seen anything like it. And even though it was all crazy, I was fucking glad that Axl had come out on top.

"Goddammit," said Axl, supporting his own weight with one arm around my shoulders, "Why would a Demon do this?"

"Axl," I said, replaying my mental image of the brick hitting the man's head, "We've gotta go."

"Right," he mumbled. Up until now, I hadn't seen him so distraught. "To the bike," he said, "Fast."

I turned around, still supporting his weight, and started to head back across the plaza the way I'd come.

"No," grunted Axl, "Could be another shooter."

"Damn," I said, the urgency of the situation boiling in my belly, "I didn't think about that."

"Yeah, they don't teach you that in college," said Axl. "We go around the perimeter, the way I came."

We rushed as quickly as we could around the circular plaza, ducking behind trees and buildings along the way. Axl's strength seemed to return to him as we hurried, and by the time we got back to the bike, he wasn't leaning his weight on me at all anymore.

The entire area had become eerily quiet and empty. The couple dozen visitors that'd been milling around had all disappeared nearly instantly, fleeing in their vehicles. No doubt many of them had called 911 already. With blood on my hands now, I was more acutely aware than ever of our need to hurry.

When we got back to the bike, I hopped on the back seat while Axl holstered his Glock, grabbing the passenger helmet and holding it in my lap. "I'll get this on later," I said, my voice tense, "Hurry!"

Just as Axl began to swing a leg over the bike, I heard a quiet whimpering sound. "Do you hear that?" I asked.

Axl turned his head and scanned the area. "Fuck," he said, shaking his head. "By the bench."

My eyes followed the direction of his gaze, and then I saw it too. The little boy who'd been flying the kite earlier was crouching underneath a wooden bench, knees pulled up to his chest. His mother was nowhere in sight.

"Dammit!" shouted Axl, pounding his fist on the bike's handlebars. He gingerly pulled his leg back over the bike, one arm across his chest, holding his injured shoulder. He moved at a half-walk, half-jog toward the bench, extending an arm to the boy underneath.

The boy reciprocated, reaching his hand out to Axl as well, when a loud shriek broke the silence. The boy's mother came running toward Axl, screaming hysterically.

"Don't touch my son!" she screamed, her voice chaotic and uncontrolled. She reached out, slapping Axl's arm, and pushed him away from the child. "Killer!" she shrieked.

Axl backed up from the woman, hardly reacting to the rain of slaps and swipes the woman was directing toward him. I could barely make out his face, but I thought that I saw a pained look on it. But as soon as I saw it, it vanished, and Axl turned back toward me and the bike, jogging as fast as he could.

Without saying a word, he grabbed his skullcap helmet from where it hung on the handlebars, slapped it onto his head without bothering to fasten the chin strap, and started the bike.

I put my hands around him, holding on for dear life as we thundered away from the Four Corners park. The bike growled between our legs as Axl twisted the throttle hard and pushed it to its limits. As we roared onto the highway entrance ramp, Axl dipped his head down, looking into one of the rearview mirrors that extended away from the bike's ape bars. He raised his fist, his thumb pointing backward, and jerked his arm to indicate for me to turn around. I twisted my head as we rode further away, and I saw flashing red and blue lights back at the park. But they weren't coming after us.

We'd gotten away just in the nick of time. We were safe. For now.

Overhead, the sun had passed well beyond the sky's apex, as the arid desert environment settled into the groove of another summer afternoon.

But for me, it wasn't just another afternoon. I couldn't get the image out of my head of the man falling. The way it'd felt when the red brick in my hand struck his head. It was unlike anything I'd felt before. A soft crunching, rigid yet organic. I'd never hurt a soul in my life, nor had I ever truly felt the desire to do so. And as much trouble as I was having coming to terms with what I'd just done in the heat of the moment, I was surprised at how little remorse I felt.

That man had come to kill us, and in this new world I'd found myself in, it was dog-eat-dog. Him or us. If I hadn't done what I did, it would've been me and Axl laying in a ditch, being discovered by the cops right now. Whatever else I felt, I felt sure of that.

I also felt sure that I'd done exactly what I wanted to. Yeah, I could've kept hiding behind the wall. Waited for the cops, and told them everything. Cleared my name. But it would've come at the cost of Axl's life. And although I didn't know what we had, I wouldn't be able to live with myself if that had happened.

A chill came over me. I had entered a new world indeed. And as we rode on the highway, it didn't just feel like we were riding away from the Four Corners park. It felt like we were riding away from everything I'd known in my life.

I held onto Axl for dear life, the pavement rushing past us just inches below my feet. The engine roared, and the wind whipped through my hair faster and faster.

CHAPTER 21: AXL

A Demon. The motherfucker had been a Demon.

It didn't make any fucking sense. Demons were based out of Nevada. Had never been interested in pushing up against our territory. I wouldn't fuckin' turn my back to one of 'em if I didn't have to, but this... This'd come out of nowhere.

Ryker and the club would be pissed to hear from me, but I had to get in touch with them. And fast.

As the bike cruised down the open highway, my thoughts drifted to Holly.

She'd killed for me, just like I'd done for her. She'd kept me breathing on this miserable fuckin' Earth for a little bit longer.

And I didn't know what I thought of that. I was grateful to still be kickin', yeah. But I'd never wanted her to get blood on her own hands. She was too good for that. My hands were too stained to ever come clean, but she'd had a chance.

Hated to see that happen. But goddamn, was she a loyal woman. Maybe even worthy of becoming an old lady.

Wasn't everyday that you found a woman that'd do something like that for you.

I reached back with one hand and tapped her on the arm. I turned my head and shouted over the wind, "Water."

I felt her shift her body, dipping her hand down into one of the bike's saddlebags, and then she handed me a canteen after unscrewing the lid for me. I took it from her and brought it to my lips, drinking deeply. The water was hot from sitting in the saddlebag all day but it still rejuvenated me. Provided my body the raw materials it needed to rebuild, for my heart to pump me full of all the blood I'd lost.

I reached behind my back again, handing the canteen back to her. She took the canteen, and then my fingers found the bare skin of her forearm.

I left my hand behind my back like that as we rode, steadying the bike with one hand only. I ran my fingers along her skin, savoring the smoothness that contrasted with the choppy, violent wind and grit that blasted into us as we rode fast on the highway.

Then I traced my fingers down toward her palm, grabbed her hand in mine, and squeezed. I linked my fingers with hers, and rested my hand in her lap behind me.

Yeah. I guess I was feeling a little sentimental or some shit. But damn, I wanted her again. One night hadn't been enough. I needed to blow off some steam, to bring her in close, and show her just how fuckin' sexy and strong I thought she was.

I looked down at the bike's console. The gas light had come on. Right now I had to pull my shit together, focus, and figure out what the hell was going on. But goddamn, I hoped that tonight we'd be able to satisfy each other over and over again, until the first rays of the sun came up.

I pulled off the highway at the next rest stop, parking next to a gas station convenience store. I hopped off the bike to let Holly dismount the passenger seat. The muscles in my legs felt stiff. My ass was killing me. I was finding out about muscles I never even knew I had.

"I'm going to the bathroom," she said. Her hair blew in the wind, beautiful against the bright blue sky. Jesus, I couldn't understand the effect she had on me. It was like fuckin' morphine.

"Alright," I grunted. "I gotta call Ryker and figure this shit out." She turned and started to walk away, but I spoke again. "Hey," I said.

I stepped toward her as she spun around, and then took her cheeks in my palms. I pressed my lips against hers hungrily, tasting her and taking in her incredible, feminine scent that drove me wild.

I pulled my lips back from hers and looked her in the eyes. "You did great back there, doll," I said. "I owe you."

She swallowed hard, seeming to have a lump in her throat. She put on a smile. "Returning a favor. I guess." She turned and walked toward the convenience store.

Sighing, I sat back against the parked bike, and pulled out my cellphone. I dialed Ryker. Fuck. This was going to be a shitshow.

When Ryker's voice came on, I didn't know if I'd ever heard him so pissed off. "Why the fuck should I talk to you?" was his greeting.

I winced as his voice blasted into my eardrum, and turned down the phone's volume. "Listen," I said, "There's shit you gotta know."

He paused, and I could practically feel the anger seething out of the phone's speaker. "What?"

"We were up north by the border. Though we were outta reach. But I took a bullet. From a Demon."

"From a fuckin' what?"

"Yeah."

He paused, growling something unintelligible. "We're clashing with Reapers here. Shit's a mess. Two incidents alone, today, at least four of their guys and one of ours."

My stomach sank at the news of yet another death in our club. "Which one?"

"Ricky."

"Fuck."

"Look," said Ryker, "I ain't heard anything about Demons getting mixed up in this melee. I'll put feelers out and call you. For God's sake, keep your guard up."

"Boss," I said, hesitating to finish my sentence. "You want us back there? I ain't tryin' to leave the club high and dry."

Ryker's voice remained angry, but took on a new tone of solemnness. "Nah," he said. "You do what you gotta do, but we don't need a deserter in our ranks."

Shit. Yeah, I'd been Ryker's favorite for a long time, but I'd crossed him bad when I disobeyed orders and picked up Holly. And he wasn't a man to take betrayal lightly.

"So what happens when this all blows over?" I asked.

"Axl, my friend," he said, "There's gonna be hell to pay. You know what this means."

I swallowed hard. I knew, alright.

If I showed up at my club again, I was gonna face a Mayhem vote. To decide whether I lived or died.

CHAPTER 22: HOLLY

I exited the convenience store, leaving the temporary air-conditioned paradise and returning to the baking outdoors. It was late in the afternoon, and the desert day had reached peak hotness.

Axl stood next to his bike, nervously shifting his weight from foot to foot. As I approached him, I saw that he held a lit cigarette between his fingers. He held the other hand over his injured shoulder, blocking the bloodied and torn bullet hole from any nosy passers-by. I felt sorry for him. But he looked even more like a handsome movie star badass than before.

Damn. If only he'd gotten picked up by a Hollywood agent instead of a dirty biker club, his life would've turned out a lot differently.

"Didn't know you smoked," I said.

"Bummed it off a guy. Only on special occasions."

He brought the cigarette to his lips and took another drag. "What now?" I asked. No one was within earshot, but my voice came out almost a whisper.

"Gotta split ASAP. Cops are gonna get our description."

"They'll be looking for a guy and a girl on a motorcycle," I said. Suddenly I felt very nervous about standing next to Axl and his bike, here in the convenience store parking lot.

Axl thought a moment. "Yeah," he said with a sigh. "Gotta ditch the bike." He sighed.

Axl finished up his smoke, grabbed a couple things from the bike's saddlebags, and said, "Come on." We left the bike sitting there and headed around the back of the store. A couple cars sat parked next to a large dumpster.

"Looks like we're driving a fuckin' cage today," Axl said.

He proceeded to jimmy open the driver's door of a crappy little Honda hatchback using a piece of wire from the dumpster. I eyed the rear employee exit of the store nervously as he did so, and it felt like days passed. But in reality he had the thing busted open and started in what was probably less than two minutes.

We got in the "cage," as he called it, and hit the road again.

I watched the passenger side mirror nervously throughout the whole ride, watching for blue and red lights in the background. They didn't come. Thank God.

Axl took us to a small town whose name I didn't know, and we found a dinky little military surplus store.

"You've gotta go in alone," said Axl, "Can't do it myself with this shoulder." His jacket was badly stained and caked with blood. Yeah. That would've been a mistake.

He sent me in with a short list, and I got us changes of clothes, a small tent, and a couple boxes of freeze-dried foods. I wasn't looking forward to eating this crap, but what choice did we have? We were now two fugitives on the run, and I guessed we weren't gonna be staying in any more motel rooms for a while.

We filled up the car and then we drove again. We sat in silence in the stolen vehicle. I could tell that Axl's mind was troubled. Not because of his hurt shoulder, but because of something else. Because of the man who'd tried to shoot us back at Four Corners. Because of who the man was. A Demon, who was apparently a member of a friendly motorcycle club, who shouldn't have been involved in this Reaper dispute.

And inside, I was troubled, too. Not because he'd been a Demon. Simply because he'd been a man.

I was conflicted, my morality gnawing at me. The clarity of mind that I'd felt earlier as we rode away from Four Corners had faded away, and I was starting to question myself more than ever. Was I becoming just like the bikers? Were these kind of justifications the way that people descended into a lifetime of crime?

I felt sorry for myself, and then for the man, and then for neither one of us. And I seemed to repeat the cycle over and over again in my head. I didn't think I'd ever be able to be like Axl. To be able to ruthlessly kill, remorselessly, for those I loved. I'd done it once but I didn't think I'd be able to do it again. And I really hoped I wouldn't have to make the choice again.

Axl finally spoke up as I watched the pavement go by outside. It was dusk outside, the Arizona sky a beautiful canvas of oranges, blues, and purples. "We camp tonight in Devil's Canyon."

I'd never heard of Devil's Canyon, and it didn't sound like a place I wanted to be. But what choice did we have?

We reached the canyon after nightfall. It was an isolated, desolate area, and the canyon was less a majestic place, more a filthy rock pit. But under the starry night sky as we pitched the tent, I finally felt a little bit of mental calmness for the first time since Four Corners. No one would find us out here. Not tonight.

Inside the tent, we lay side by side under a couple of rough blankets that'd come with the military surplus tent, our bodies not touching.

Then, Axl's hand wandered over mine, and onto my stomach. He pressed his hand against the hard muscles of my belly, and then began to slide his hand up to my breasts. Turning onto his side to face me, he cupped my left breast in his hand under my t-shirt, the rough calluses on his palm scratching against my nipple.

"Babe," he said, "I fuckin' want you so bad right now."

Inside the tent, it was pitch black and we couldn't see each other's faces. But if he'd been able to see mine, it would've been a frown. I wanted him, too, for him to fill me up again just like he'd done at the motel. I wanted him to give me everything, and to lose myself in ecstasy for just a while. But I was exhausted, and it just didn't feel right after what I'd done to that Demon earlier.

I pushed Axl's hand away from my breast. "Can you just hold me?" I asked.

Suddenly his demeanor turned cold. He grunted. "Whatever," he said. I felt him turn away from me instead of putting his arm around me like I wanted him to. Soon, his breath became regular, rising and falling in a sleep cycle.

I lay on my back, staring straight up in the darkness. Sleep came slowly, and when it finally overtook me, my dreams were nightmares.

CHAPTER 23: AXL

When I returned to the wakeful world, green light was filtering through the camouflage fabric of the tent. For a fucked-up minute, I couldn't remember where I was.

Then I felt the pain in my shoulder and everything came back to me. I rolled over to where Holly had been lying next to me, but the woman was gone.

I vaguely remembered blowing her off when she didn't wanna fuck. Shit. I felt like a real asshole over that. But I'd needed a release so fuckin' bad after yesterday.

And God, I still did now. My cock was rock hard under a pair of boxer briefs that we'd picked up at the surplus store. As I lay on my back, I reached down and wrapped one hand around my stiff tool. Fuck, I was so hard, but no way was I gonna pressure her. I wasn't a fuckin' brute and I could tell she had shit on her mind. But I had to get a release.

I spit on my hand, reached under the fabric of my boxers, and wrapped my hand around my erect dick. I began to jerk my hand up and down the length of my shaft.

In my mind I pictured Holly there next to me, naked and on her knees, begging me to take her.

Jesus, I wanted to have her again so bad. I'd never felt like this about any chick before. I thought back to the way her firm ass had felt pressed against my hips as I plowed into her, balls deep. I squeezed my hand harder around my cock and jerked faster, recalling how her perky little breasts had felt in the palms of my hands as I'd exploded inside her. And it pushed me over the edge.

"Oh, fuck," I said under my breath. My dick began to pulse, shooting its creamy, pent-up load all over my t-shirt and the blanket. But I didn't give a fuck. It felt so fucking good to get off to her. Next time it had better fucking be inside her.

I took off my bloodied t-shirt and used it to clean up, and realized how hot it was in the tent. Jesus. I pulled my jeans on, opened the flap, and stepped outside into the hot, bright blue morning.

I felt a clarity of mind that I hadn't had in the last couple days. I was pretty sure that this bullshit with the Demons was being driven directly by fucking Vargas. That fat piece of Reaper shit was reckless enough to try turning the Demons against the Sons.

My train of thought was interrupted by Holly. I saw her standing by the cage, and she was topless also. She held one of our water jugs and she was scrubbing her shirt between her hands. She hadn't noticed me yet, and I watched her beautiful body as she worked. Her skin was light and pale in the morning sun, her waist slender and her breasts tight against her chest. God, she was gorgeous. My cock stiffened in my pants again, and I felt like no amount of release would be enough. Trying to drain my balls with her around was like trying to drain the fucking Niagara Falls.

I walked toward her and the cage. When she noticed me approaching, she turned toward me and crossed her arms over her chest. I grinned at her.

"Don't stop, darlin'" I said. I could see her eyes roaming over my bare chest and six pack. But then I saw them turn to the wound on my shoulder, and she furrowed her brow, still crossing her arms and hiding her breasts.

"How's the shoulder?" she asked.

I extended my arm and rotated my shoulder, stretching and testing the muscles. There were no more sharp pains, just a dull ache. "Better," I said. "Fucking glad the bullet didn't lodge. Could've gotten real nasty."

"Does it feel infected?"

I shrugged. "Nah. Never had a problem with that kinda thing." It was true. I'd gotten pretty fucked up on a few occasions, but I always bounced back fast. My body was a tank that just couldn't be stopped.

"Hmm," she said, still looking at the wound disapprovingly.

I stepped toward her, moving to put my hands on her waist, grinning at her. But, she turned her cheek and moved away. "Whatever," she said, and I realized she was mocking what I said to her last night. I just cracked a smile at her. I wasn't even mad. She looked hot as fuck.

"You gonna get dressed?" I said.

"Actually, yeah. Would you mind?"

"Not at all." I grinned again.

"Ugh. Turn around."

I laughed and turned away. But then I turned back, just in time to see her pulling the still-wet t-shirt over her head, sliding it down over her chest. She pulled it down quickly and slapped my arm. "Axl!"

I laughed. "Damn girl," I said. "That thing better dry out fast or I'm not gonna be able to think about anything else today." I stared at her nipples, outlined in the damp fabric.

"Enjoy it while it lasts, pervert," she said.

"Alright," I said, using all my willpower to pry my eyes away. "Seriously, though, we've gotta make our next move. And I know what it is."

"What?"

"Vargas. That fat guy back at the junkyard. Remember him?"

"Yes."

"This shit ain't gonna end 'til he's gone. History. He's a warmongering freak and the shit between our clubs is gonna get worse long as he's around."

"You're going to kill someone else?" said Holly. Her expression was one of worry.

I paused before answering. "Yeah. I got to."

"Isn't that just going to fan the flames?"

"Don't think so," I said. "All Reapers are shit, but their VP ain't as shitty as Vargas. Worked with him before, a practical guy, not a fuckin' maniac. Someone the Sons could work with. And from what I hear, he wouldn't pursue vengeance on the Sons if something happened to Vargas. Hates the guy himself, wants to take over the Reapers."

"And," I added, "Could be my only chance to get back in my club's good graces."

Holly frowned. I could tell she didn't like this at all. But it wasn't a choice. "Do more people really have to die?" she asked.

"Yeah," I said, nodding. "Yeah they do."

CHAPTER 24: HOLLY

I didn't want any more violence and killing. All night, I'd had nightmares about yesterday. In my head, I kept going back and forth about what happened. Whether I'd been justified in what I did. Whether I'd be able to live with myself, knowing that I'd taken a person's life. Whether I'd have been able to live with myself if I *hadn't* done what I did.

I was conflicted, and I was more than a little afraid of what I was capable of.

This wasn't the direction I'd envisioned my life taking. And Axl was not the kind of man who would have fit into my old life.

But this was my new life and there was no going back. College, graduation, and my documentary, which were the most important things to me just a week before, now seemed a distant memory. When the Reapers had come after me in my own house, it changed everything.

Before that, I still could've somehow gone to the cops. But after Axl rescued me, going to the cops would've meant turning him in. And I couldn't make myself do it then.

Now it was too late even for that. Now, going to the cops would mean turning myself in as well.

I was in this deep. Way too deep to think about getting out now. And against my own best interests, I was falling for Axl. I was changing. And I didn't know who—or what—I would to be when I came out the other side.

It scared me and I tried to fight it. I looked in his eyes, feeling the breeze pass over my damp t-shirt. It cooled my body, providing a much-needed respite from the heat.

"Axl," I said, "More death can't be the answer."

He shook his head. "You're wrong, doll. It is the answer."

"Why? Look where it's gotten us. Living out of a stolen car, in a crappy tent in the middle of the desert."

"Holly," he said, "It's either out here, or six feet under. I told you before. This life chose me, and it chose you too. Adapt or die."

"I can't stop thinking about yesterday," I confessed. "It's really bothering me. Like, a lot." I felt like I might cry, but I steeled myself and resolved not to let it happen in front of Axl.

He sighed. "Walk with me," he said, and reached out. I put my hand in his, and we started to walk around the perimeter of Devil's Canyon.

"Lemme tell you about the first time I killed a man," he said. It felt really weird to hear him say that. And even weirder to identify with it.

"I met the Sons when I was sixteen. Just got my license, and my foster dad got me a cheap Japanese dirtbike. Rode it everywhere. Loved that fuckin' thing. Anyway, I started hangin' out with other guys who rode bikes, and kept crossin' paths with Ryker and another young cat named Dash. Found out they were part of an MC—the Sons.

They had a place to belong. I didn't. But they brought me in, and that was somethin' I'd never had before. I got to be tight with them.

"They started bringing me along on deals. I was a prospect. One day we had a drug drop-off with another crew. Don't remember which. Anyway, I was posted up on the roof of a building, keepin' an eye on the deal. Shit went south, and one of their guys pulled out a knife. Looked like he was gonna shank Dash in the back. Real fuckin' bitch move. So I pulled out the old revolver they'd given me, and I lit the fucker up."

I let the story sink in before speaking. "And how did it make you feel?"

The rocks crunched beneath our feet as we walked. When I almost lost my footing, Axl yanked me back up. Even the pull of my entire weight didn't throw him off balance.

"Shitty," he admitted. "Real fucking shitty. You gotta be a monster to not feel that," he said. "Like Vargas. He's a fucking psychopath." He continued, "But it was either him or Dash. And maybe more of our guys too. And eventually me. That's the way it works on the streets. Them or you."

His words made sense, and sounded just like what I'd been thinking yesterday. It made me feel a little better, but it also scared me that I was thinking the same way as a grizzled biker. I kept trying to fight the feeling. "Why not just walk away from it all?" I said.

Axl shook his head. "And do what? Live alone and flip burgers all day? I got nothin' except the club."

"It's not too late for you," I said. "What if we fix this somehow. Get back to normal life. Move far away."

Axl chuckled. "It *is* too late for me, darlin'. I got too much blood on my hands." His smile slowly faded. "But you don't. For you, it's not too late. You ain't gonna forget what happened yesterday, but don't let it eat at ya. Remember what I said. Them or us. That guy woulda killed me and then you. It was self defense. Believe me."

"What about the cops?" I asked. It freaked me out to think of my face on a wanted poster. I felt paranoid, sure that they would find us.

Axl rolled his eyes. "What about 'em? Ain't no evidence on you, and let me tell you somethin'. You think cops give a shit about a couple bikers killin' each other? Well, they fuckin' don't. They care long enough for the public to forget about it. That's why we're out here. We ride out the shitstorm, and soon it'll be just another unsolved mystery in a cardboard box, in the basement of the police station. Ain't nobody gonna suspect a damn thing about you."

His words made sense. For the first time since it'd happened, I felt some peace of mind. What I did didn't make me a monster. It was them or us.

"Is that what you want?" he said. "I can keep you safe while I take out Vargas. Get this shit over with. Then you can go back home."

I stopped walking and turned toward him. "What do *you* want?" I asked. "What is this, anyway?"

We were still holding hands, his right in my left. He took my other hand too. "I don't know, doll," he said. "Do what you gotta do. I ain't tryin' to drag you down to my level. But if you stay, then as far as I'm concerned you're my old lady."

I stood there, holding his hands, the sun beating down on us. We were all alone in Devil's Canyon, no one around us, no one to influence my decision either way. I weighed the options. Wait for this to blow over and go back home and never see him again, or take a chance on this. To let the lifestyle choose me. And to be his old lady.

In that moment, I changed, and I knew what I'd become. Not a ruthless killer, but a stronger woman. One who'd do what she had to do to protect those she loved.

Loved? Did I really think that?

I felt pretty sure, but I couldn't bring myself to say it. Not quite yet.

I looked into his eyes, full of life and energy, and marveled at his beauty. Even out here, completely in the rough, he was a gorgeous, strong man. He didn't need anything or anyone. He was just living life by his own rules. They were chaotic rules, but they weren't evil ones.

I wasn't going anywhere.

"Well," I said, "You gonna kiss your old lady or what?"

CHAPTER 25: AXL

I slid my hands up her back, over her shoulders, and my fingers meshed with her soft, thick hair. I held the back of her head in my hands as if were precious gold. And then, I kissed her deeply. My Holly.

My old lady.

The intensity of the kiss left my lips feeling napalmed. God, she set every part of my being on fire. I wanted her so fucking bad.

But I was also terrified of corrupting her. The shit I said to her made sense to me, and I knew it was true in the club lifestyle. But shit, to be honest with myself, I didn't know if it was true for a good girl like her. I didn't know if a person could just go from college student one day to killer the next, and not be eaten alive by it.

All I knew was that I was willing to do anything it took to make sure she never had to spill another drop of blood again. That shit was for people like me, who were already ruined. Not for a spring chicken like her.

When our lips parted, she was breathing heavily. "Axl," she said, "I need you right now."

Just hearing those words nearly made my cock tear through my Kevlar jeans. I fucking wanted to, worse than anything. If she'd said it ten minutes ago, I'd have been all over her. But after this conversation, I had to focus. Had to stay alert. If I was gonna hit Vargas, I had to do it fast before the situation evolved.

"Babe," I said, "I wanna tear you apart right now, but it ain't the time. We gotta get you somewhere safe while I handle this."

The lust in her eyes almost brought me to my knees. That look could destroy a man.

And if I got soft, I knew it would destroy me.

We packed our shit back into the car, fast, and left Devil's Canyon behind us.

As we rolled down the highway, she pulled her phone out from her backpack and turned it on. "I've gotta say something to my parents. With me being gone and what happened on my street, they probably already filed a missing person report."

I cringed at the thought. Despite the reassurance I'd given to her earlier, the cops could fucking take us down right now. Yeah, this shit would eventually blow over like I said, but right now, we were in their crosshairs. More attention was the last thing we needed.

"Yeah," I said. "Fuck. You better make up a good story."

"No signal," she said.

We kept driving and she kept trying her phone. I headed toward a border town near Cali, where the NOMAD compound was. NOMADs were guys without a club affiliation. And those guys owed me. They would keep her safe while I fucked up Vargas.

After twenty or thirty minutes, she said, "Signal's back." And almost at that exact same time, I felt my phone going off in my pocket, buzzing again and again, as it caught up with a huge backlog of missed texts.

I jammed one hand in my pocket and pulled it out. I handed it to Holly. "Read the messages to me," I said, keeping my eyes on the road.

She took my phone from me and started poking and swiping through it.

Then she gasped. "Oh my god," she said. The tone of her voice sent a shiver down my spine.

"What?" I said, forcefully.

"It says, 'Demon hit inside job. Watch your back.'"

I felt like a sledgehammer had gone off, ricocheting through my chest and head. I wrenched the wheel to the right, and the car careened into the dirt shoulder. We were buffeted by the road's roughness. My head struck the ceiling hard as the car screeched and skidded to a halt in the dirt. The cars that had been following us swung out wide, and the drivers gawked at us through their windows.

"Gimme that fuckin' thing," I said, snatching the phone from Holly's hands. I looked down at it, and it said exactly what she'd read to me. The "Sender" field said: Dash.

I roared. "Shit!" I slammed my hands down, snapping a piece of plastic off the center console of the car. Out of the corner of my eye, I saw Holly flinch.

"Fuck, fuck, fuck!!" I screamed. I was losing control, and the only thing that stopped me going utterly fucking nuts was Holly's calming touch on my arm. I breathed hard, grinding my teeth together, trying to wrap my head around what I was reading. An inside job against one of your own guys was the biggest "Fuck you," the ultimate, unforgivable crime. If, for whatever godawful reason, a club had to take out one of its own guys, it was done by a Mayhem vote. Legit. Honorably.

And although I knew I might face a Mayhem vote when I went back to the club—*if* I went back to the club—that ain't what this was.

This was something else, and I knew right away what was happening.

Lynch. That dirty, rotten fuckin' dog carcass had to be at the core of this. Wasn't anybody else in the club who woulda had a reason, or the balls, to do this.

"Fucking Lynch," I said.

"The bald guy? The guy who tried to grab me back at the junkyard?"

"Yeah," I fucking growled. "That fuckin' piece of shit. We gotta get you to the safe house. Then I'm gonna fuckin' rumble. It's gonna be a bloodbath."

Holly's expression was solemn. But she didn't protest like I thought she might. Instead, she nodded.

"I understand," she said. "You gotta do what you gotta do." She was starting to understand how this worked.

I nodded, heat rising off my body in waves.

Nobody double-crossed me and lived to tell the tale. Nobody.

CHAPTER 26: HOLLY

The air conditioning had burned out in the shitty little Honda we'd stolen, so we rode with the windows down. The evening air was hot and humid, and although it whipped through my hair, it provided no relief from the scorching heat.

Axl's knuckles blanched against the hard plastic steering wheel. He was squeezing it hard, and I could tell that wires of tension were tightening throughout his body. I felt the same way. My whole body was uncomfortable, my mind anxious.

"Axl," I said, "This isn't about the video anymore, is it?"

"No," he answered, staring straight ahead as he hit the accelerator and passed a car on the left. "Never was."

"They're using me as a pawn in their game." I was starting to understand how the game worked.

Axl nodded. "A Reaper came by the club. Said they were after you. Hardly even gave a shit about the tape. The tape incriminated both our clubs, it gave us no leverage on them. But you gave them leverage on us."

"Because they saw you protecting me."

"Yeah. They find your weak spots. Pick at the scabs until they bleed. Anything your enemy cares about is a weak spot."

I hesitated for a moment but then spoke. "Why did you care about me?"

"Told myself it was about protecting an innocent. Sons code says to protect 'em. But..." he trailed off.

"But what?"

"You made me feel somethin' I hadn't felt before."

I reached over to the steering wheel and placed my hand on his.

"What happens if they find out I'm your old lady now?"

Axl took his eyes off the road for the first time in at least an hour, and looked right at me. "What do you think?"

Shit. To the Reapers, I was just a button to be pressed, a weak point to exploit. That made me mad. A club that'd use a woman to manipulate a rival club couldn't have any honor. I'd pretty much thought of all bike clubs as criminal enterprises up until now. But now I was starting to see the shades of grey. How there was a code of honor even on the streets, among criminals.

"Where're you taking me?" I asked.

"Cali border hideout. NOMAD compound."

"What the hell does that mean?"

"Unaffiliated bike chapter. They're good guys. I trust 'em."

"You're sure?"

Axl looked at me again. "Would I lie to you?"

I nodded slowly, giving him my trust. He hadn't let me down and I didn't feel like he was going to.

We got to the NOMAD compound after dark. Somehow, lady luck had been on our side, and we made it halfway across the state without any cops picking up on our plate, which had to be reported stolen by now.

The compound looked like a bunker. A long, flat, nondescript concrete building that looked like it was made to withstand a direct assault. As we pulled up, the lights were down and the place looked deserted. But as soon as our front tires hit the property line, huge spotlights came on and flooded the car like day. I shielded my eyes, and saw that five or six guys with huge black rifles had come out of nowhere and were checking us out. When they saw it was Axl in the driver's seat, the floodlights went down and they waved us in.

Axl took us around the perimeter of the compound, toward the opposite end of the complex. "Entrance is on the other side," I said.

"Yeah. If you wanna get in, you gotta go all the fuckin' way around. Safer that way. If you ain't supposed to be here, they just light you up before you have a chance. Look," he said, pointing to the compound roof. In the moonlight, I could make out a shadowy figure on the rooftop, holding the same type of assault rifle. "Reapers ain't gonna touch you here."

I believed it.

As we slowed to a stop on the opposite end of the compound, an unmarked, un-windowed door swung open and a big burly, older guy with a white beard emerged. He looked like a big biker Santa.

Next to me, I noticed Axl's face light up. It was the first time he'd cracked a smile since seeing me topless in Devil's Canyon. He swung the door open excitedly and practically leapt out of the car. I swung my door open, too, and stretched my muscles as I got out.

"Big Mikey!" said Axl, his voice warm and excited. The two men swung their arms wide, and embraced each other in a massive bear hug. I couldn't help smiling to myself. After the endless piles of shit we'd sifted through in the last week, it was really nice to see Axl in a moment of pure happiness. I walked around the car, toward the two men.

"Axl, my boy, it's been too long!" Big Mikey broke their embrace and held Axl at arm's length, looking him up and down, pride on his face. "You ain't changed a fuckin' bit!"

I interrupted the reunion. "Are you his dad?" I asked.

Big Mikey and Axl both looked at me and burst into laughter. "I ain't his dad, darlin', but he's as good as my son." He smiled one of the most genuine smiles I'd ever seen. "And you are?"

"Holly," I said. "I'm Axl's... old lady."

Big Mikey looked at Axl, an expression of amazement on his face. "Never thought I'd see the day."

Axl shrugged, a cocky smile on his face, and turned his palms up in the air. "I know a good one when I see one," he said, winking at me.

Big Mikey turned toward me, and started making a sound like a combination of "awww" and "ohhhh," cocking his head and holding his arms out. He smothered me in a bear hug and planted a kiss on my cheek, his beard scratching my face. "You got a good man right here," he said, releasing me. "Axl's never let me down. And any old lady of his is a welcome guest here—always."

"Thanks," I said, a big dumb smile on my face. Big Mikey seemed to beam constantly, and it was impossible not to smile back at him. I liked him already, and I felt like I could trust him.

His expression did turn solemn, though, as he looked back at Axl. His eyes darkened, and for some reason it made me sad to see.

"Axl, my boy," he said. "We've heard rumblings of war between the Sons and Reapers." Axl nodded, his smile tapering off as well. "Yeah," he said. "Shit's a mess right now, Mikey. I need a favor."

CHAPTER 27: AXL

"Anything for you, brother," Big Mikey said. I fuckin' hated to see him so concerned. Mikey was always the sunshine that lit darkness.

But I pushed the thought outta my mind. Behind his jovial eyes and friendly exterior, there was one of the toughest motherfuckers I knew. A man who could handle anything. I trusted the man with my own life, and I trusted him to keep Holly safe while I dealt with Lynch and did what I shoulda done a long time ago. With Lynch to deal with now, Vargas was gonna have to fuckin' wait a little longer for his turn.

"We'll talk," I said, "First, let's get her a room." Big Mikey nodded, not questioning me. There was a solid trust between us that I seldom found in this fucked-up world.

We dropped off Holly in a guest room that was spartan but clean. Then me and Big Mikey walked and talked, and I filled him in on the shitstorm. "I need you to watch my old lady, keep her close, while I take care of this shit," I said. But, I kept my mouth shut about Lynch. Didn't say a word to Mikey about what I planned to do. That was a secret that I couldn't share with anyone. Not even Mikey.

Big Mikey nodded at me when I finished talking, no longer smiling. "Aye," he said. "We'll keep 'er safe, boy. Go to her now, stay the night. You look like hell. Ain't gonna be good to the Sons if you fall asleep at the wheel."

I still felt wired, and I was jonesing to get back on the road, despite my exhaustion and still-injured shoulder. Probably would've, too, if anyone else had told me to sleep it off. But coming from Big Mikey, the suggestion carried more weight, seemed smarter in my mind. "Yeah," I said, "You're right. I leave bright and early."

Bike Mikey nodded. "Come here, my boy," he said. I gave him a crushing hug, man-to-man. I turned and walked out of the room without saying another word to him.

Jesus Christ, I needed a fuckin' shower like nobody's business. I beelined straight for the dorms, caught up with a couple NOMAD brothers from back in the day, and borrowed a towel and some garb. Then, I hit the showers and washed away all the blood, sweat, and grime that had accumulated on me in the hot, dusty desert. My shoulder was healing up nicely and hurting less. Thank fuck for that. I couldn't afford to waste any time getting' patched up in an ER.

When I was finally clean, I toweled off, put on the borrowed clothes, and headed back to Holly's room.

When I entered, she was lying on top of the bed, one towel wrapped around her body and another around her wet hair.

"Same idea, eh," I said, grinning at her and shutting the door behind me. Holly smiled, but instead of answering me, she stood up and let her towels fall to the floor.

126

Blood rushed into my cock, and I felt lightheaded. The effect this girl had on me was just fucking unbelievable.

"Goddamn girl," I said, stepping toward her, "Where'd you get this body? It just drives me fuckin' wild." I crossed the room and put my arms around her waist, pulling her in close. I felt her breasts press against my hard abs through my shirt, her nipples pebbled. My cock throbbed in my pants, and I pulled her into it. She gently ground her hips against me, feeling my hardness.

All she said was, "Show your old lady how much you want her." Oh lord, was I going to show her. I couldn't fucking believe that we'd only fucked once. I needed to be inside her again.

I grabbed the collar of my t-shirt with both hands and pulled it over my head, revealing my hard, muscled physique. Holly ran her hands over my forearms, bulging with muscle and hard veins developed by years of riding and violence.

I was gonna fuck her harder than she'd ever been fucked. I wanted her to be fuckin' shellshocked and think of nothin' but me 'til I got back.

I pushed her away, toward the bed, and she fell back with a giggle. "Show me how strong you are, mister," she said with a gleam in her eye.

I grabbed her by the shoulders, sparing her none of my strength, but using the utmost caution to not hurt her. I turned her around, so she faced away from me, toward the bed. "I'm gonna take you from behind," I said, my voice a low, deep growl.

She twisted her head and looked back at me. "Yes, sir," she said with a shy smile. I pushed my head forward, driving my lips into hers. I kissed her ferociously, pressing my hard, thick cock into her ass and running my hands up her sides. They found her breasts instinctually, and I cupped them in my hands, letting her femininity flood through my senses. I couldn't wait another goddamn second to be inside her.

I put one hand around the back of her neck, and pushed her head down into the mattress. She arched her back, her animal instincts perfectly complementing mine. Her ass pressed against my cock, and I felt my heart pound as my eyes hungrily took in the sight of her most private parts. Still pressing her head and neck down into the mattress, I brought my other hand to her clit and began to rub it softly. She moaned, crying out in muffled pleasure as I circled the nub with my fingers. She was so fucking wet and ready for my cock, and nothing on Earth could've prevented me from giving it to her.

I used my fingers to open her folds, and pressed the tip of my cock against her opening. I felt her hot wetness slide over my cock as I pressed myself deep inside her.

The sensation was unparalleled. No fucking drug, no fucking booze, no fucking money, no fucking other woman in the world held a fucking candle to the sheer pleasure she gave me. I thrust in and out of her hard and unprotected, her tightness squeezing hard against me, dripping wet with desire.

"Fuck yeah, baby," I grunted, slamming my cock hard and deep into her. I put one hand around her hip, using it to pull her into my cock even harder, even faster.

"Oh Axl," she moaned, "Fucking take me, I'm yours."

"Fucking right you are," I said, my voice husky. I kept my rhythm steady, but increased my pace as I felt my orgasm building inside me. "You're the only woman I need in this goddamn world."

"Fill me up," she begged, her voice on the verge of a plea.

"When I'm good and fucking ready," I said, breathing hard. Her pussy was so fucking good for my cock. It felt like it was made just to pleasure me, just as tight and wet as I needed it to be.

She brought one hand up to her clit, and started rubbing it hard. As she did, I felt her muscles tighten and contract against my cock, her body doing everything in nature's power to get me to explode inside her.

"Oh fuck," she said, "I'm gonna come."

Those words pushed me over the edge. "Me too, babe," I said.

She whimpered, and cried out, "Oh, God!" as her orgasm shook her body.

My cock exploded inside her at the same time, pulsing in sync with her, draining my virile seed into her tight little body. "Fuck," I grunted. I needed my cock as deep in that pussy as it would fit, needed to fill her with every drop I could muster.

As our simultaneous orgasms subsided, I pressed her to the bed hard, collapsing on her back, my cock still hard inside her.

"Holly," I said, breathing hard, "You are sexiest fuckin' thing I've ever laid my eyes on." I let my cock slide out of her, covered in my cum and her wetness.

I laid my head against a pillow, and pulled her in close, nestling her body against mine.

She turned her head around and planted a kiss on my lips. "You do me so good," she said. "And you protect me so good. I didn't think guys like you were real."

I chuckled under my breath. "A hundred percent real, darlin'."

She yawned. "Are you gonna stay here tonight?"

"Yeah," I said. "Leaving in the morning. But tonight I'm all yours."

CHAPTER 28: HOLLY

We should've gone to sleep after that. We were both on the verge of physical and mental exhaustion, but finally spending time together was exhilarating. We lost count of the orgasms between us, as Axl took me over and over again.

We caught up on what felt like a lifetime of being apart. We'd barely known each other a week, but the connection was so strong, so indisputable, that it didn't even seem strange to me. Being his old lady and entering this new world just seemed like the natural progression of my life at this point. Did I want to finish my degree and my documentary? Hell yes I did, and I intended to. But right now, things felt right and I didn't want to miss a minute of Axl.

We finally fell asleep in each others' arms as the sun started to rise. When I finally woke up, it was past noon and Axl was already gone. I hoped he'd been able to get some sleep. It scared the shit out of me that he was willingly going into harm's way, and I wanted him to have all his wits about him.

After I woke up, I lay awake in bed for a while texting on my phone. I'd finally been able to reach my parents. They were mad, but thank God, somehow hadn't heard about the incident with the guys in the van, nor had they filed a missing persons report. They just thought I was off gallivanting with "that biker scumbag" and were more angry than worried. This time, their anger was a relief. I hated to lie to my parents, but I had to make up an excuse. If I'd admitted that I actually was with the "biker scumbag," who knows what bloodhounds they might've unleashed on me.

I was still laying in bed when there was a loud rap on the door. I pulled myself out of bed with a sigh and answered it.

"Mornin', sunshine! Sleep well?" said Big Mikey. He looked back to his jolly self today. Either he had total confidence in Axl to take care of business, or he was hiding his actual concern.

I smiled. "Hi, Mikey," I said. "Just fine, thank you."

"You just let me know if you need anything. At all," he said. He gave me another cheerful smile. "Head down the hall and to your right to the mess hall when you're ready. One of our cooks will whip up somethin' tasty for you."

"I really appreciate it," I said. "Hey, Mikey," I continued.

"Yeah?"

"Axl's gonna be good. Right?"

He nodded slowly and replied in a tone that inspired genuine confidence in me.

"Known him since he was a kid. No one I'd trust more to make it out in one piece."

I mustered a smile. "Thanks again, Mikey. I'll be by the kitchen soon." He gave me another smile. "See ya."

I changed out of my pajamas and followed the directions Mikey gave me to the compound's mess hall. It looked like a diner, with a grill behind a long counter with stools, and a bunch of booths and tables. The place was mostly empty, with only a couple tables occupied. The kitchen, though, smelled divine. I caught a whiff of burgers cooking. I'd been planning on asking for a stack of pancakes, one of my favorite comfort foods, but now I was torn.

I sat down at the counter and realized there was a laminated menu tucked into the napkin holder. I giggled softly. The idea of a biker hideout having its own chef and a real menu was cracking me up. I wasn't complaining, though. It was way better than the Sons clubhouse, where the only thing to consume was alcohol.

An Italian-looking guy in a chef's hat came out from the kitchen. "Whatcha having?" he asked.

"Pancakes?" I said. I had to go with pancakes.

"You got it," he said, and disappeared again into the kitchen.

As I sat waiting for my food, a pretty but plain-looking blonde girl entered the mess hall. She was wearing a blouse, jeans, and high heels. Much more dressed up than I was. She looked around the room, and I thought she seemed nervous. Then she walked up to me at the counter.

"Anybody sitting here?" she asked.

"Nope," I said. She pulled out the stool next to me and sat down.

"I'm Ashlynn," she said, and held out her hand. "It's nice to meet you."

I shook it. "Holly," I said. I was trying not to look completely out of my element. "Are you an old lady?" I asked her.

Her eyes widened and an amused expression came over her face. "Dammit," she said, "Knew I should've put on more foundation this morning."

We both cracked up laughing. "Sorry," I said. "I didn't mean it like that."

"Just playin'," she said, giving me a wink. "Nah, I'm not an old lady. Not yet, at least. You think I'd be wearin' this ridiculous get-up if I didn't have to?"

I had a feeling this girl was what the bikers called a "hanger-on." But I wasn't about to say that to her face.

She continued. "What about you? Haven't seen you around before."

"Yeah," I said, trying to sound casual. "I'm Axl Archer's old lady."

Her eyes widened again, and she looked visibly impressed. "Axl Archer from the Sons of Chaos?"

I nodded yes.

"Damn, girl," she said. "Every biker chick this side of the border wants to hook up with Axl Archer."

That was news to me. But I wasn't exactly surprised. I had no doubt that Axl caught women's attention wherever he went.

"Well," I said, doing my best to sound modest, "I happen to believe they're the lucky ones." I grinned at Ashlynn.

She giggled just as the chef came back out of the kitchen with my pancakes. They were topped with a square of butter just like in movies. They were picture perfect, but for some reason I wasn't feeling very hungry anymore. "Thanks," I said to the chef.

"Ooh," said Ashlynn, "I'm gonna get some too, they look so good."

"Help me with mine," I said, pushing the plate toward her. "No way I can finish them."

I sat there chatting with my new friend, nibbling on the pancakes, but my appetite seemed to have left me. I pulled out my phone from my pocket a couple times during the meal, checking it for a text or call from Axl, but there was nothing.

I hoped he would make it back soon, and all the shit with the clubs would be over with. But I had a feeling it wouldn't be that simple. In the club life, it never was.

CHAPTER 29: AXL

I left around 9am. Only caught about 4 hours of shut-eye, but having Holly all night was all the healing I needed. Your average Joe mighta felt drained and wasted after a week of violence and a full night of fucking, but me, I was a new man.

I left her tucked in under the thin sheets, running my hands lightly over her naked body one more time. If I didn't come back, I wanted to make sure I croaked with her on my mind.

I thought I might be starting to feel something. Like, something real.

Love.

Part of me thought to wake her up and tell her, but I couldn't make myself do it. Maybe I was afraid she'd love me too and then lose me.

I skipped breakfast and went straight to the garage. Mikey's mechanics had taken care of the jacked car last night. Scrubbed the VIN, threw on a new plate, and repainted it. And apparently fixed the A/C as a courtesy. Good fucking thing, too, 'cause it was gonna be in the hundreds today, and I had a six-hour drive ahead of me back to Redstone.

Once on the road, I hit up Dash on my cellphone. I needed someone I could trust if I was gonna pull this off.

"Yo," I said.

"Axl, man. Was getting worried about you."

"I'm good. I'll be in town at 3:30. Need you to meet me at the Rock Tavern. And bring Red with you."

"Yeah, alright," said Dash. "We'll be there."

I slammed the phone down on the seat next to me, and cranked up the A/C and the radio. Nothin' like highway radio stations to get you through a boring fuckin' drive.

Pissed me off to still be in this fuckin' cage, though. Minute I could, I was gettin' a new bike and puttin' this piece of shit in the crusher.

I got back into town right on schedule and parked the cage behind the Rock Tavern, our old haunt. If shit was on one of the guys' minds and he wasn't at the clubhouse bar, you almost always found him at the Rock Tavern.

Dash and Red were waiting in a booth when I stepped inside. But instead of entering with my usual swagger, I kept my head down.

Our haunt or not, couldn't be too safe in times like these.

I joined the guys at their booth with a tip of my head.

"Axl, buddy, Jesus. Glad you made it in one piece," said Dash. He seemed nervous. Red nodded. "Heard about the Demons. That's fucked up, man."

I looked at Dash. "Does he know about the other thing?"

Dash shook his head no.

"Tell him what the fuck you told me," I said.

Dash looked apprehensive, reluctant. "You sure?"

"Tell him."

Dash turned to Red, next to him. "Reapers aren't working with the Demons. The Demon hit was an inside job. From within the Sons."

"Wager my life it was Lynch," I added.

Dash looked at me and gave a single nod. "Yes," he said. "Lynch."

Red looked hard at Dash, his eyes bulging. "How in the fuck do ya know this?"

"After we heard the VP was shot up in Four Corners, I did some digging on the streets. Had a hunch. Put pressure on a couple Demons." He shaped his fingers into a gun and pointed them at his skull, clarifying the type of "pressure" he meant. "Lynch has been unhinged lately. We should've seen this coming."

Red nodded slowly. "All the guys see what's goin' down between you and Lynch," he said, looking at me. "Ain't a secret."

"Don't say 'you and Lynch,'" I growled in a low tone. "I ain't on the same level as that shithead."

Red nodded. "We know that, boss."

"Update me on the Reapers," I said.

Dash just shook his head sadly, and Red replied after exhaling air slowly through his lips.

"Drive-by at the Bunny Ranch Strip Club two nights ago. Bastards caught four of our guys, two still in critical condition. Knocked Striker off his bike the day before that, busted up his leg real good."

"Fucking savages," I said. My blood boiled.

"They're pushin' up against our territory real good," said Red, shaking his head sadly. "Only a matter of time before we see something big. A bombing or some shit. This's been a long time comin', but they're makin' all their moves now."

Dash nodded. "I agree."

"What's their end game?" I said.

Dash replied. "Break the Sons charter. Mass surrender and patch-over."

I gritted my teeth. "Day I wear a Reaper patch is the day they put my rotting corpse in the ground."

"But this shit with Lynch," said Red, "Could *really* tear the club apart."

I knew he was right. I'd seen shit like this before. An external enemy like the Reapers was dangerous, but an internal enemy was what killed morale and set men against one another. If we were gonna take out Lynch, we had to do it fast, and clean.

"Goddamn," I said, shaking my head. "Never fuckin' thought it'd come to this. I gotta clear my head." I whistled loud and threw a hand in the air to signal a waitress. "Be a doll, Jack shots all around."

The waitress brought us each a tall shot glass of whiskey. "Put 'em down, boys. That's an order," I said.

We put the shot glasses bottom-up, and I felt the gears in my head start to spin the way I needed them to.

"VP," said Dash, "Say we gather evidence, call a Mayhem vote on Lynch, and lay everything out for the club to vote on."

I shook my head no. "That fucker's too deep up Ryker's ass right now," I said. "Ryker ain't thinkin' straight. We call a Mayhem vote on Lynch, and more than likely it's me that ends up on the chopping block after the shit I've pulled."

Dash nodded, understanding my drift.

"We hit him hard, and fast. Make it look like an accident. Make it look like the Reapers got him."

"Yeah," said Red. "Lynch's the most wanted man in the club. He's been out there on the front lines, hittin' them everyday. They want his ass and nobody's gonna question if he takes a bullet to the brain one night."

I nodded, the plan coming together in my mind. "First thing's first," said. "We get rid of Lynch, then we hit Vargas hard enough to send the Reapers back home, lickin' their wounds."

Dash and Red nodded in agreement.

"Dash," I said, "You been closest to Lynch. When's he gonna be off-guard?"

Dash paused, thinking. "At his pad," he said. "Fucker's got a nice vacation home down in Phoenix. Wife and kids are out of town 'til next week. He's there every Thursday."

"Wife and kids gone—you fuckin' sure?" I said, my eyes narrowing. "Sick and fuckin' tired of innocents getting' caught up in our bullshit. We see any sign of a woman or child, we turn around and go home. No debate."

Dash nodded. "I'm sure. His old lady has the kids in Florida right now, up with the in-laws. Two thousand miles away. Lynch will be alone."

I nodded, looking back and forth at Dash and Red. "Hold this in complete confidence," I said. "One word of this gets out... I'll cut both your throats myself." I couldn't fuckin' imagine Dash or Red saying shit. And I sure as hell couldn't imagine cuttin' their throats. But I wanted shit to be crystal clear.

Both men nodded solemnly, not speaking.

"Then it's decided," I said. "I'm layin' low just outside of town. Can't show my face at the club now. Same time here tomorrow, we figure out the details."

"We'll be here, boss," said Red.

"Stay safe, buddy," said Dash, looking into my eyes. He held eye contact just a little longer than normal. "Catch you here tomorrow."

Dash and Red got up and left. I sat there for a few minutes in thought, then signaled the waitress for another whiskey. This one I sipped slowly. One hand on the glass, and the other hand on the Glock on my hip. As I drank, my eyes scanned around the room.

Couldn't be too careful.

CHAPTER 30: HOLLY

The next morning, I was under the weather. I'd gone to bed without eating much, and when I woke up, I felt like I was coming down with a stomach flu. Lovely. I wished I was back home with my roommates, or at my parents' house. Being sick while away from home was the worst.

Fortunately, I at least had my new friend Ashlynn to keep me company. I was lying in bed reading the news on my phone when she came knocking at my door.

"How you feeling, girl?" She asked, cracking the door and poking her head through.

I sighed. "Come in, Ash," I said. "Been better." I was trying to lie as still as possible, because every time I moved it felt like my guts were sloshing around inside me.

"Awe," she said, putting her hand on my shoulder. "What say I help you get dressed and we get some chicken noodle soup?"

I mustered a smile for her. "Okay, let's give it a shot."

We made it down the hall to the kitchen and sat at our usual spot at the black-and-white checkered countertop. The Italian cook, who I now knew as Luigi, brought out two bowls of steaming hot soup with saltines. "Feel better," he said with a sympathetic smile.

The soup was tasty and rejuvenating, and my stomach began to calm down as Ash and I sat, talked, and ate.

But halfway through our meal, a dangerous-looking group of five or six men burst into the mess hall, loud and raucous. They commandeered two tables near the entrance. One of them, a greasy-looking kid who looked like a bad impression of Elvis, kicked back in a chair and threw his muddy boots on the table. The stench of alcohol reached my nose from across the room.

Next to me, Ashlynn groaned quietly. "Don't give 'em attention. Just finish your soup and we'll go."

"You know these guys?" I whispered back.

"Yeah. Mean drunks that come by here every week after dropping off crank for their club."

"Which club?" I asked, keeping my voice low.

"Demons."

I nearly spilled a spoonful of salty broth and noodles into my lap. "Oh my God," I said, feeling my skin prickle. "A Demon tried to kill Axl. And me."

Ashlynn's eyes widened in alarm. "What?!"

I put the spoon down into my unfinished bowl of soup, quietly. "We need to go," I whispered. "I'll explain later."

Ashlynn nodded.

We stood up and walked toward the exit. I looked straight ahead, not making eye contact with the boisterous men. But I could tell they noticed us. Before we got to the door, the young greasy-looking one crossed the room and blocked our path.

"In a rush, ladies?" I looked into his beady eyes, which sparkled insincerely. His skin was a mess and his teeth were crooked and yellowed. His breath stank of booze and cigarettes.

Ashlynn, who'd been following behind me, stepped up next to me. "Get outta our way, Ford."

"Nah," he said with a dirty grin, "I don't think so. How you been, baby? And who's your little friend?"

"I'd watch your fucking mouth if I were you," Ash said. "She's Archer's old lady. Fuck with her and Big Mikey'll cut your puny dick off."

"Shut up, bitch," Ford snarled.

A week ago, I'd have been intimidated by this guy's crude behavior. But by now, I'd seen worse. My intuition told me this guy was a little bitch under a fake "tough guy" persona.

"Back off," I said. My lips seemed to be doing the talking for me. "Get outta the way, or Axl will kill you like he killed your buddy at Four Corners."

Ford's eyes swiveled to me, angry. But behind his anger, there was confusion. I had a read on him. My street smarts were catching up to my book smarts. He was just a scared little piglet, a follower who didn't really know what the hell was going on.

"The hell you talkin' about?"

By now, we'd caught the attention of the other Demons, and another one walked up to us. He was tall, ripped, and had a hard jawline and a military-looking high 'n tight haircut. Clearly the leader. Ford's posturing diminished as the bigger man approached, his behavior changing from aggressive to deferential. It was easy to tell who was really in charge here.

"Hey boss," said Ford, looking up at the taller man, "This bitch was saying—"

The taller man spoke over Ford, cutting him off. "I heard. Now git." He flicked his head, ordering Ford to scram, who obeyed after giving me and Ashlynn one last dirty look.

"Listen," said the man, lowering his voice, "I heard about that bullshit with your old man. Listen. I couldn't give less of a fuck about the Sons of Chaos," he said, "Ain't got no particular love or hate for 'em. But there's nothin' I fuckin' hate worse than a sell-out." He moved in closer toward us, lowering his voice even further so his guys wouldn't overhear. "The Demon who shot up your old man was paid off. We don't love the Sons, but we also ain't tryin' to start a war with 'em. He was a lone wolf."

I nodded. "We know it was a Son who paid off your guy. I don't think Axl blames your MC for this."

He nodded and stood up straight. "Good. But understand. After I heard about this bullshit, I put the squeeze on a couple of my own guys. Suspected they knew somethin' about it. Gave me a name."

I nodded. "Axl knows it was Lynch who paid off your guy."

The man looked briefly confused and shook his head. "Well, that ain't the name I heard."

My heart beat faster. "What'd you hear?"

"Name I got was Dash."

I felt like someone had pulled a fire alarm in my head. Ash must've sensed it, 'cause she said, "Hol, what's wrong?"

"Shit," I whispered. My head was pounding. "That's Axl's buddy. The one he went to meet yesterday. The one who gave him Lynch's name."

"Oh, shit," said Ashlynn.

The man's expression hardened. "Smells like a set-up to me," he said.

"Shit," I repeated. "We gotta go."

The man nodded. "Hope your old man makes it outta this."

"Come on," I said to Ashlynn, and rushed out of the mess hall with her behind me.

We stood in the dorm hallway. "I've gotta call him," I said, pulling my phone out of my pocket. All I could think about was Axl unknowingly walking straight into a trap, and getting betrayed by Dash. I had a horrible, sinking fear that I wouldn't see him again. I almost felt—no, *did* feel—like I'd rather be there instead of him. I'd never felt so protective of any guy before, and I was terrified that something might happen to him. Did this mean I loved him?

But there was no time to dwell on feelings. I dialed Axl and held the phone to my ear. It went straight to voicemail without ringing. I tried again, with the same result.

"Ash," I said, my voice starting to rise in panic, "I've gotta get outta here and get to him."

"You gotta talk to Big Mikey," she said. "This way!"

She rushed down the hall, leading the way to Big Mikey's office, and I scurried behind her. When we got to the door, she barged straight in without knocking. Big Mikey was sitting behind a big mahogany desk, looking down at a financial ledger book, glasses resting on the bridge of his nose. He looked up in surprise.

"Just what-" he began, but Ash cut him off.

"Mikey," she said, puffing, "Listen to Holly."

He looked at me, cocking an eyebrow.

"Axl's in danger," I said breathlessly. "And he's not picking up his phone."

"Whoa," said Big Mikey, "Slow down. Start from the beginning."

I explained to him as quickly as I could. But before I could finish, he shot upright out of his chair.

"Stop right there," he said, "Getting my guys, and we're going. Jesus, he didn't tell me the Demons were involved in this, or I woulda kicked 'em the fuck outta here."

"It's good you didn't," I said urgently. "If we hadn't run into those Demons, we'd never have known. But you have to take me along."

Mikey shook his head. "Can't do that. Axl asked me to keep you safe, and that's what I'm gonna do."

"I can handle myself," I said. "I won't get in your way. I'll go crazy if I'm waiting here."

He sighed. "Women these days," he muttered. "Alright. Come. But do exactly as me and my guys say."

I nodded. I was pumped up with adrenaline, and I wasn't paying any attention to my aching stomach anymore. I just had to get out of there.

We had to find Axl and warn him before it was too late.

Big Mikey crossed the room, his pace quick, and opened the door. "Let's go," he said.

CHAPTER 31: AXL

The next day, I was waiting for the guys at the Rock Tavern. Same time, same place. It was quiet this afternoon, not a lot of folks drinking. As if all was calm before the storm.

I ordered a double whiskey on the rocks that I was nursing when they showed up. I needed to be on fuckin' point. We only had one chance to get this right.

I tipped my head to Dash and Red as they slipped into the leather booth opposite me. "Afternoon, boys," I said.

"Afternoon, boss," said Red. Dash gave me a solemn nod, and we all leaned in close.

"So, boss," said Dash, "How do you want to do this?"

I smiled. That was the question that'd been on my mind all night.

There were just so many fuckin' options, I didn't know which one to pick. A bullet to the head. A bullet to the heart. Chloroform overdose. Or maybe just an old-fashioned beating 'til that fucker stopped breathing. Each method was just so special in its own way, but it was a tough decision, 'cause that cunt deserved 'em all.

"Well," I said, "I've been thinkin' about that. And while I'd love to mess him up real good, we gotta make this clean."

"Agreed," said Red.

"Ain't nobody can find a trace. So we're doin' this with a good old bag over the head. Plus," I added, "I'm tired of being caked in blood all the damn time."

Dash laughed softly. "Understood."

Red nodded.

"Lynch swings by his place every Thursday at eight," Dash said, "Before hitting the strip club."

I swirled the whiskey around in my glass, mixing it up with the melting ice. Then I tipped it to my lips and threw my head back. The liquid burned my throat on the way down, and I loved every second of it.

"Good," I said. "We'll be waitin' for him when he shows up."

"What about the body?" asked Red.

"I don't want a single fuckin' trace of that cunt left anywhere on this planet," I said. "And you know what that means."

"Do we?" asked Red.

I nodded. "If there's somethin' strange in your neighborhood, who you gonna call?"

"Mr. Clean," said Dash.

"You're goddamn right," I replied. "Clean's the only motherfucker I trust to get every last piece of Lynch outta there. When the wife and kids get back from Florida, won't even be a stain to remember their old man by."

Red grinned. "I like how you're thinkin', boss."

I nodded. "Dash," I said.

"Yo."

"You got a copy of the keys to his place, right?"

"Right."

"Then we meet here tonight, seven o'clock. Parking lot. We take one cage to his place and stake out his living room. Lights out. And we wait for him."

Red nodded. "Let's do this."

"It's on," said Dash.

I showed up in the Rock Tavern parking lot at six-fifty in the hatchback cage that I'd jacked. Sat in the driver's seat while I waited. Damn, I missed the girl. Wished I could take her to bed for the night instead of dealing with fucking Lynch. Wished I could make love to her all night, exploring every inch of her body. There was still so much more of her to conquer, to own, and I wanted all of it.

Dash showed at two minutes 'til on his bike. He locked up his helmet and walked across the parking lot to my cage. I unlocked the passenger side and he got in.

"You ready to do this?" I asked, my voice hard as steel.

"Yeah," he said. "But Red can't make it."

My eyes narrowed. "What d'ya mean, 'can't make it?'"

"A couple guys got messed up in a rumble today. Reapers. He's our only medic right now. Working on them back at the clubhouse. Sends his regards."

Fuck. Me and Dash would have to make this work. But I didn't fucking like starting this off one man short.

"Alright," I said after considering. "Let's roll."

We hit the road and got to Lynch's place about half after. It was an old strong adobe house in the suburbs of Mesa. Flat, short but wide, and the color of clay. The street was quiet, the horizon blue and orange, colored by the setting desert sun. The neighborhood was peaceful, oblivious to the violence that was about to go down.

We parked the cage one street down from Lynch's place, and walked to the property. We went around the back, where there was a small, dead lawn and a big inflatable pool. Must've been his kids'. Damn, I felt bad for the poor little fuckers, but I didn't have a choice. Their dad was the worst kind of scumbag. God knew I might be doing his kids a favor by getting rid of him. I carried a crowbar with me, and I crammed it into the frame of the sliding glass door on the back patio. As I wedged the door open, I said, "You ever met Lynch's old lady?"

"Yeah," said Dash. "She's alright."

"Good," I said, thinking back to my childhood in the foster system. "'Cause she's about to be a single mom."

I pried with the crowbar, grunting as I applied force, and the sliding glass door finally popped open. "Hold this," I said, passing the crowbar to Dash. I grabbed the door handle and pulled it hard, wrenching the door open.

We stepped inside, and I surveyed the living room. Typical family feel. Pretty clean. Not what you'd expect from a biker. I wondered how Lynch had become such a piece of shit. From seeing his place, you'd have thought he was a totally normal guy.

Dash followed behind me, looking around.

"Nice," I said, tapping my boot on the tiled floor. "Easy clean-up if things get messy."

"Yeah," said Dash. From behind me, his voice sounded unusually tense.

"Everything good, man?" I said, looking around the room for the best hiding spot.

"Yeah," said Dash. "Hey VP," he said. "Come here and look at this."

I pivoted around on one heel.

The last thing I saw was Dash raising his arm, and bringing the crowbar smashing down onto my head.

CHAPTER 32: HOLLY

Our convoy rumbled down the highway, seven or eight bikes in front of us. I sat in the passenger seat of the chase vehicle, a van that followed the bikes in case one broke down. Its cargo area was outfitted with tie-downs for two bikes, and it was also outfitted as a makeshift ambulance. These NOMADs really knew how to prepare.

I was worried sick about Axl after what that Demon told me. I'd been calling him nonstop, but none of my calls were getting through. They all went to voicemail, and now I'd completely filled up his inbox. I'd blown up his phone with texts.

Nothing. Nothing was getting through, and I had no way to reach him. I was horrified at the thought of losing the only man that I'd ever truly wanted to be with. I thought back to how it felt to be in his arms, to be snuggled up against him at night, and to have the security of knowing that he'd do anything—absolutely anything—to protect me. I'd never met a man like that before and I doubted I ever would again. I wanted him to be safe and healthy, and I wanted us to be together.

152

"Where do we look first?" I asked Big Mikey.

"When we chopped that cage y'all rode in, we threw a GPS tracker on it," said Big Mikey.

"You what?"

"That's SOP," said Big Mikey. "Standard operating procedure. We like to keep tabs on the vehicles that pass through our shop."

"Well," I said, "I hope it pays off. Do you know where it is now?"

"Yeah," he said. "Mesa suburb. Been sitting on a residential street for the last half hour. Got my guy back at the compound researching points of interest around the area. We'll find out what's around there and get to the bottom of this. Try calling again."

I dialed Axl again with the same result. "Nothing," I said.

Big Mikey's face was grim. "Alright. Hang tight 'til we get there."

We rode in silence for about ten minutes, then Big Mikey's cell phone rang. "Yo... Apple Grove and Campbell Street. Got it." He hung up the phone. "We've got an intersection on the vehicle."

My heart thumped hard in my chest, and the next fifteen minutes passed as slowly as an eternity. Finally, as we approached our highway exit, Big Mikey passed the bikes and led the way into the suburbs. The streets got smaller and smaller until we were in the twists and turns of a small neighborhood. The sun was going down, but it was still light out. I was worried about the convoy of bikes attracting attention, but Big Mikey didn't seem worried about it, and I trusted his judgment.

Finally, I saw a street sign that said "Campbell," and we turned onto it. "There!" I blurted, pointing to the now-repainted hatchback. I unbuckled my seat belt and started to open the passenger door before Big Mikey even stopped the van.

"Wait—" he said, but I jumped out of the van the instant it lurched to a stop, and rushed across the street to the car.

It was empty—no sign of Axl.

Big Mikey jogged up next to me, cupped his hands against the glass of the car, and looked inside. "Damn," he said. "Alright, lemme make a call." He dialed on his phone again. "Yo. We're here but car's empty... Yeah... Results from the database? Addresses to check out? I can't just go knockin' on every door on the street... Okay, great." He hung up and looked at me.

"We got a lead. The Sons's road captain lives one street down."

"Road captain?" I said. "Shit, that's Lynch!"

"Oh, fuck," said Big Mikey, his face dropping. "Let's go."

Big Mikey and I walked toward the next street on the sidewalk, moving fast, leaving the chase van parked where it was. A couple bikers rumbled on the street next to us, turning their heads back and forth and scanning for any signs of danger. Big Mikey kept his right hand on the gun under his jacket.

We passed a man and woman walking their dog, and they eyed us worriedly, walking off the sidewalk into the dirt and slinking around us. I was definitely beginning to understand biker psychology. The power was addicting. It felt good to have people step out of your way.

But I didn't have time to ponder the subtleties of power dynamics right now. All I wanted was to find Axl safe and sound.

"That's the one," said Big Mikey, pointing to a short, tan adobe house. We rushed across the street, almost running. There were no cars in the driveway. I jumped forward to run up the steps to the front door, but Big Mikey put out one arm and held me back. He drew his gun and stepped toward the door, cautiously. He reached out to the handle and wiggled it. "Locked. Around the back."

My whole body was tense, and I was afraid of finding the worst. The house was too quiet.

I followed Big Mikey around into the backyard. "Door's been forced," he said. "Stay put 'til I give a signal. I'm goin' in."

I stood nervously on the back porch, crossing my arms over my chest and trying to steady my breathing. Two more bikers came around the side of the house on foot, and entered where Big Mikey had gone in. I heard scuffling and yelling inside, but it didn't sound like a fight. Finally, I heard, "*Shit!* Clear!" Then, my heart sank when I heard the word "*Medic!*"

Big Mikey came bounding out of the house.

"He's hurt bad. But he's breathing."

CHAPTER 33: AXL

When I woke up, I had no fuckin' clue where I was. My head was pounding something fierce. A million times worse than any hangover. Never felt anything like that in my goddamn life.

My first reaction was to call out for Holly. Had she been with me? Did these fuckers get their hands on her?

My second reaction was to start swinging, and I caught a motherfucker right on the jaw. Blood sprayed out of his busted lip, and droplets spattered onto my face and lips. Not fucking again. I spat, trying to clear out my mouth. I tasted the unmistakeable, metallic flavor of blood.

"Fuck!" A voice shouted. "Hold him down."

I tried to swing again. If I was going down, I was taking this motherfucker with me, whoever he ways. But I felt my hands being held down at my sides. "Fuck!" I screamed. My vision was blurred, and I couldn't fucking see shit.

"Axl! It's me," said a soothing female voice.

"Holly?" I said, bewildered. I tried struggling again, but I was completely pinned down.

"Babe, it's me," she said. "You're alright."

156

My cloudy vision began to clear. I looked side to side. I was in some kind of compartment, lying on my back. Holly sat to my left, and a biker I didn't recognize sat to my right. He was holding a towel to his mouth, and it was stained red.

"Where am I?" I said, dazed.

"Axl, it's me. We found you in a house. Bleeding on the floor." She reached out and pushed my hair up, caressing my forehead. "Tell us what happened."

I was still woozy. "Who's this motherfucker?" I stumbled over my words as I spoke.

"The medic," said the biker gruffly. "Don't fuckin' hit me again."

What the fuck? A medic?

"Where am I?" I repeated.

"In the NOMAD ambulance," said Holly. "Mikey's driving. Tell me what happened," she repeated.

I tried to think. Suddenly, it came back to me. "Shit," I said weakly.

Dash. That coward. The pain of the betrayal I felt was a thousand times worse than the pain in my head.

"Went to get Lynch..." I said. "Dash... Double-crossed me."

The medic biker spoke up. "Don't move your head. Can't believe you're still kickin' after taking a blow like that."

"Yeah," I said, my voice trailing off. "He smashed me with a crowbar."

"Axl, babe," said Holly. "I ran into a Demon at the compound. He said Dash was in on it. Tried calling you a million times."

"Damn," was all I could muster. Fucking technology and I did not get along.

"I have to get back," I said, "and find Dash."

The medic shook his head. "You ain't goin' anywhere for a while, man. They left you for dead. Can't believe you even made it. Here comes a poke."

I grimaced as I felt an IV being inserted into my arm. I was covered in ink, but I fuckin' hated IVs.

"We'll figure it out later," said Holly. I strained my eyes to see her without turning my head. She looked so damn beautiful, even with her face covered in worry.

"Be back," said the medic. He stood up and shuffled around the cramped van cabin, heading for the passenger compartment, leaving me and Holly alone.

"Babe," I said, "Kiss me." Holly leaned down, and gave me a gentle peck on the lips, as if she were afraid to hurt me with a kiss. I must've looked pretty fucked up.

"Axl," she said, "Is this all worth it?"

"Can't let Lynch and Dash get away with this... They gotta pay."

"But babe," she said, her voice a mixture of concern and frustration, "This is the second time you've cheated death since I met you. You won't keep getting lucky."

"Worked for me so far," I said, trying to muster a grin. The muscles in my cheek felt like they didn't want to move, but it must've worked because Holly smiled back weakly.

"Axl, what if we just go? Go far away from here, and don't look back."

I was getting annoyed. Not only did I have to defend myself from my friends and enemies now, I also had to defend my choices to Holly?

"Everybody gets busted up sometimes," I said stiffly. I felt lightheaded, and a wave of nausea passed through my belly.

I guess I could see her point. But there was no fuckin' way I could let this slide. It went against everything I stood for. "Is that what you do?" I asked. "Just run away from your problems when shit gets rough?"

She stopped stroking my forehead, and sat back. "These aren't normal problems. Normal problems are putting food on the table, finding a babysitter for the kids, or working late. This is fucked up, Axl."

I grunted in disapproval. "Running ain't my plan."

"What *is* your plan?"

"Revenge," I said. The word tasted sweet on my tongue, rolled off my vocal cords buttery smooth. I was gonna fuck those guys up. It was the end of the fucking line for them.

Holly was upset now. "How much more blood has to be spilled?"

"You don't have to be involved," I said softly. "In fact, it's better if you're not."

"And what happens after that? Doesn't this mean something to you? Don't I mean something to you?"

"Yes," I said, pursing my lips. "And we can talk about it. But don't fuckin' tell me how to handle my own business."

"What if you don't make it out this time?"

I thought for a moment. I didn't fuckin' like thinking about death and I tried not to do it. I always made shit work out. But I felt closer to death now than I ever had before, and I couldn't deny it. Maybe I was fated to go out fighting. Probably was.

"It doesn't matter," I said, "I don't care if I come back alive."

Holly didn't respond, and the rest of the ride passed by in awkward silence.

I wasn't lyin'. I didn't give a shit if I made it out alive, long as I gave those two fuckers their due. Sure as hell didn't have a club to go back to either, so what did I have to live for?

I tried not to pay attention to the voice in the back of my head. The one that was telling me that Holly was what I had to live for.

CHAPTER 34: HOLLY

It was nearly two o'clock in the morning when we got back to the NOMAD compound. They wheeled Axl in on a stretcher and took him to the infirmary. Big Mikey and I walked with him and talked to the "doctor," a sinewy-looking guy who'd been a field paramedic for the IRA for two decades.

"Concussion, fractured orbital," said the doc in his Irish accent, "but he'll recover. Miracle for sure."

Axl was sleeping peacefully when I returned to his bed. I hated to see him weak, hurt, and vulnerable. It was so unlike the strong, capable man that he was. I felt an instinct to stay and protect him, but I was absolutely beat.

"Get some shut-eye," said Big Mikey. He looked worried about me.

"Promise me you'll keep him safe while he's out."

"Don't you worry about that. I've got my four best guys posted at the door. Nobody can touch him here. Kicked those Demons the fuck out, too."

I reluctantly returned to my room, undressed, and fell asleep before I could even brush my teeth. My dreams that night were nightmares.

The next day, I slept in until past noon. When I woke up, it was only because Ashlynn had come knocking on my door again.

I was awakened by her pounding, and I stumbled out of bed and across the room. Light streamed in through the windows, which I'd forgotten to cover the night before. It was beautiful outside, and it felt like a new day. I hoped that the windows were open at the infirmary and the beautiful day was having a healing effect on Axl. I was anxious to get down to the infirmary to see him.

"Holly! It's me!" Ashlynn's voice came through the door.

I opened it, and she walked in, spry and bushy-tailed as ever.

"Oh my god," she said, rushing her words. "What happened yesterday? I heard Axl's in the clinic. Are you okay?"

I sighed. "Lemme get dressed and go check on him. Then we can talk."

I had to borrow more clothes from Ashlynn. I'd just about given up on having any semblance of style or dignity since this entire adventure had started.

We checked on Axl, who was still out cold. "Come back tonight," said the doc, "He might be up by then."

Ashlynn and I left the infirmary and went to the mess hall, but my stomach was hurting again and I wasn't hungry.

"Damn girl," she said, "You coming down with some kind of stomach flu?"

"I don't know," I said. "This has been going on for a few days now." I hadn't ordered any food of my own, because Ashlynn had ordered pancakes to share. I drizzled some syrup on them, but it only seemed to make me feel worse.

Halfway through the meal, when I was telling her about how we found Axl, I started to heave. I ran into the mess hall bathroom and barely reached a toilet before I started to throw up. Ashlynn held my hair back. I honestly didn't know what I'd have done here without her.

"Girl, is this 'cause of last night?"

I wiped my mouth with my sleeve and shook my head. "No," I said, "I don't think so."

"Did you eat something bad?"

"Just what we had together. And you didn't get sick."

I flushed the toilet and moved to the sink to wash up. "I hope this gets better before I end up in the infirmary, too," I said.

Ashlynn paused, not speaking, seemingly in thought. Then she spoke. "When's the last time you got your period?"

I turned the water off, and looked down in thought. I hadn't even been thinking about that.

"Uh, I guess it's late," I said. "Should've started a day or two ago."

"Do you think there's any chance... You know," said Ashlynn, her voice trailing off at the end.

My heart pounded at the thought. I sure as hell hadn't planned on getting pregnant. There was no way. I was on the pill, and I'd managed not to miss one throughout this whole ordeal. That was something I took *very* seriously.

"I'm on the pill," I said slowly. "I don't see how that could've happened."

"Well, it's not a hundred percent," said Ashlynn tentatively.

Now I was getting freaked out. Going on the run with Axl was one thing, and I'd almost come to terms with the fact that my life had irrevocably changed. But now in addition to being a biker's old lady, I was going to be a knocked-up college dropout? I almost couldn't wrap my mind around the idea. All my life I'd been brought up to do the exact opposite of that.

"I just don't know," I said. I tried to reassure myself in my head. "I don't see how it's possible."

"They keep pregnancy tests in the clinic," said Ashlynn. "It's a... thing that comes up every once in a while around here."

I laughed woefully. "That would really be the fucking cherry on top," I said. "Walking into there and asking the doctor for a pregnancy test in front of Axl. The entire compound will be talking about it."

Ashlynn laughed quietly, and then said, "But seriously, I'll go get one if you want. I'll tell 'em it's for me."

"You'd do that for me?" I said, amazed.

"What are friends for?" said Ashlynn. "But you'll owe me for this." She laughed.

"Okay," I said. "Jesus. I can't believe this is happening. It has to be negative. Has to be."

I went back to my room and waited for Ashlynn to come back from the infirmary. When she got back, she came in my room without knocking, where I was nervously sitting on the edge of the bed.

"Got it," she said, waving a white plastic wrapper in her hand. "Good thing I went to, 'cause your boy's up."

I perked up, almost temporarily forgetting the mess I was in. "How is he?"

"Seems good," said Ashlynn. "He was checking out my ass."

I turned red.

"Just kidding," she said. "He's a hunk of man, though, even laid up in bed like that."

"I know," I said.

"Alright hon," said Ash. "Go pee on this and bring it back."

I went to the bathroom down the hall and did as I was told. When I was done, I wrapped the small plastic stick in toilet paper and clutched it tight in my hand, not daring to look at the results.

I brought it back to my room. I held my hand out and uncovered the plastic stick.

"Tell me what it says," I told her.

She bent over to look.

"Oh, shit."

CHAPTER 35: AXL

When I finally woke up in the infirmary, the sun was already setting. I didn't know what time it was and the doc was nowhere to be seen. My head felt like a fuckin' Mack truck was parked on it. I was getting real sick of waking up feeling like a train crashed into my head every damn day. Maybe Holly was right, I should've called it quits right then and lived out my days on a golf course in Florida. Sure would've been more fun than this.

I reached up and felt my face. There was a big bandage over my right eye, but otherwise everything felt intact.

Can't lie. Even though I was fucked up, I felt a little proud. Like a fuckin' bull. That piece of shit Dash had beamed me with an iron crowbar and left me for dead, and not a day later, here I was, gettin' better. Gettin' ready. Ready to fuckin' find him and finish the job that he didn't.

When I got my hands on him, there wouldn't be a second chance for him. He wouldn't wake up later. In fact, no one would find him at all. And what I was gonna do to him was a fuckin' tickle compared to what I was gonna do to Lynch.

Five or ten minutes later, I heard talking at the infirmary door. Big Mikey came waltzing in, just like nothing had ever gone down. But the expression on his face was one of relief. Didn't think the bastard was capable of worrying, but I guess I understood. I would've been distraught as fuck if this shit had happened to him.

"Hey, sunshine," he said. "You are one lucky motherfucker."

"Not lucky," I said, trying to put on an air of bravado. "Just built like a fuckin' bull." I forced a grin.

Mikey smiled back. "Yeah, you fuckin' handled that. What was it, a crowbar?"

"Yeah," I said, my smile dropping. "Beaten senseless by my own fuckin' crowbar." It pissed me off. I'd paid good money for that thing.

Big Mikey sat down on a stool next to the bed where I lie, and he put a hand on my shoulder. "Where's your head at in all of this?" He asked me.

I gritted my teeth, my lips contorting with displeasure. "You know me. So you know where it's at," I said.

Big Mikey nodded. "I wanna see these guys go down, too. But I overheard what your old lady said to you, son."

I shrugged. "Don't eavesdrop on me."

"*Overheard*," he emphasized. "Look, all I'm sayin' is that you've managed to have an ace in the sleeve when it's counted. Twice recently. But there comes a time when a man needs to be smart, and to assess the risks he's takin' on."

"I've assessed," I said, "I've assessed and I'm goin' the fuck in."

Big Mikey was choosing his words carefully. It was plain to see that he was torn up about the whole thing. Getting sentimental over me. That was the bad word. It was dangerous. And weak.

"Look son," he said, shifting his tactics, "I just don't wanna see you rush into some foolhardy mission and get fucked up."

"I'm ready for whatever happens," I said. "I've got nothin' left now. No club, no honor, no friends, no family. Ain't got shit."

"That ain't true," said Big Mikey. He was motioning with his hands as he spoke, his palms up, almost as if he were pleading his case to me. "You've got your old lady. You've got me. And you've always got the NOMADs. You've got a spot in this place anytime you want."

"Thanks, Mikey," I said. "But I ain't got many options left now. This is gonna be a one-way mission, man."

Mike's eyes narrowed and his expression was one of worry. "What does that mean?" he asked.

"There's only one way to get those fuckers who crossed me. And that's at the Sons clubhouse. They ain't gonna let their guard down anywhere else."

Mikey tipped his head, looking at me with disapproval. "You ain't sayin' what I think you're sayin', are you?"

"Yeah," I said, "I am."

The truth was, I was way more fuckin' conflicted about it than I was lettin' onto. Mostly because of Holly. She was the only person who'd made me feel a damn thing in years, and I hated the idea of leaving her all on her own. Shit, by now she might've been marked for life. Even if I fuckin' smoked Lynch and Dash, if I burned out doin' it, Sons weren't gonna protect her. Reapers'd have open season on her.

But what choice did I have? I couldn't bear the thought of leavin' her, but I also couldn't bear the thought of not makin' Dash and Lynch pay for their crimes.

"So what's the plan?" asked Mikey. He blew air out from between his lips as if he were deflating, giving into the inevitability of my determination.

"Take a week or two to get patched up here. Get back to a hundred percent. Then find a way into the club and start shootin' when they least expect it. Dash and Lynch only. Won't hurt another fuckin' soul in that club. Not even Ryker. We had our differences but he loves the club, man. I do too. They're my brothers."

"Yeah," said Big Mikey. "But you'll never get outta that alive."

"I'll do my best to figure out a way," I said. "But if I can't, I can't. You'll take care of my old lady if I go down, right?"

I could see tears clouding up Big Mikey's eyes, and I had to swallow hard. Fucker was chopping onions in here.

"Yeah man, we'll keep her safe. But fuckin' find a way to come back," he said. He got up and headed for the door without another word, no longer trying to argue with me. We both knew the chance of me coming back was slim to none.

I was doing what I was best at. Projecting confidence and strength. Inside, I was torn the fuck up. I didn't want to leave Holly. But I had to take out Dash and Lynch.

I heard that voice in the back of my head again, telling me she was worth it. But I shut it down. I didn't have a choice.

I was going in.

CHAPTER 36: HOLLY

The next few days were quiet at the NOMAD compound. The doctor kept Axl on bed rest in the infirmary. I went to visit him every morning, and although he was getting better, he seemed distracted. I tried to cheer him up and lighten the mood, but I couldn't stop thinking about our last conversation. About him being prepared to go on a suicide mission.

The first time I visited him, I almost spilled the beans right then and there, told him that he was a father now and I was a mother. But I couldn't bring myself to do it.

I wanted him to want me, wanted him to give up the lifestyle of mayhem that he had cultivated and that had brought him to his knees. But with each passing day it seemed less likely.

I began to think about running away. I was absolutely sure that I wanted to keep the baby. That was never a question in my mind. But I'd be damned if I'd let my own child be raised in this kind of place.

Something—someone—was going to have to give. And it was going to be me or Axl.

Without the baby in the picture, I don't know what I might've done. Once it was in the picture, though, it forced a decision. Either Axl would have to get his shit straight and leave the lifestyle, or I'd split. There could be no half measures.

About a week after I found out, I decided I had to talk to Ashlynn before making a decision. She was the only one here who I could trust, who I could confide in. I sure as hell wasn't about to have this conversation with Big Mikey.

One afternoon Ashlynn was hanging around the compound and I went to find her. "Let's walk and talk," I said, "I need to work this out."

We walked around the perimeter of the compound, which wasn't exactly a nature trail getaway. More like a dirt sidewalk right up against a barbed-wire chainlink fence. But it would have to do. There wasn't anywhere else to go to clear your head.

"I don't know what to do," I confessed to Ash as we walked. We strode side-by-side, our young skin glimmering with perspiration in the desert sun, not yet reddened and grizzled like the skin of the old ladies that'd been around the compound for years.

"I know how you feel," she said. "I wouldn't want to bring a kid into this life either."

I looked down at my feet, placing one in front of the other as we circled the compound. "It's not just that," I said, "I mean, maybe if I tell him, he'll change his mind about this whole plan."

"You told me about it," said Ashlynn. Her voice was soft but serious. "Sounds like he might not come back from that."

I nodded, swallowing hard. "Yeah. I don't know if telling him would change anything. He doesn't need this shit on his mind. He's gotta focus."

"Girl," said Ash, "I think you've gotta do it."

"Why?"

"He's so obviously into you. I bet he's torn the fuck up about this plan. He's in a bad place right now. He needs you, and that means you need to be completely honest with him."

"Do you think it'll change his mind?" I asked.

"Maybe," she said. "I can't predict the future. But he should have the facts before this goes down."

We walked in silence for a few minutes while I considered what she said.

Finally I said, "Ash, I really appreciate what you've done for me."

She scoffed. "Didn't do anything I wouldn't have done for anyone else."

"I mean it," I said. "I was all on my own when we got here and you showed me the ropes."

"You're welcome."

"You really think I should do it?"

"I do."

I slept on it, but the next morning I decided to take Ash's advice to heart. I went to the infirmary to find Axl, but he wasn't in his bed.

"He's on the upswing," said the doc. "Went down to the gym this morning."

"Thanks," I said, and went back into the hallway. I found stairs to the basement, which was a musty, industrial subterranean cavity with walls made of stacked cinder blocks. It felt unfinished, not final, and I hoped that Axl's decision about this mission would be the same way.

I found him in the weight room, which just had a bench press, weight rack, and a big mirror on the wall. He lay on the bench, pumping iron.

For a minute, I totally forgot about my troubles, forgot about the tough conversation ahead. I just watched him as he lifted. His body was beautiful in action. His arms and chest were thick and powerful, overcoming the heavy weight of the iron bar and plates as if they were feathers. The skin on his arms and shoulders was taut, his youth and virility on display. Jesus. I hoped that I looked half as good as he did.

When he finally racked the weight, I spoke up. "Axl," I said across the room.

He sat up in surprise. His face was still bruised, but the bandages had been removed and he was starting to look normal-ish again, which made me happy.

"Didn't see you there, babe," he said with a grin. "Felt so much better this morning. I'm on the mend."

I forced a thin smile. "I'm happy to hear that," I said. I hesitated, trying to muster the willpower to speak. Finally, I did. "There's something I need to talk to you about," I said.

"Shoot," he said.

"There's no way to beat around the bush," I said. "I'm pregnant."

I sucked in a nervous breath and waited for his reply.

CHAPTER 37: AXL

Pregnant.

That word fuckin' floored me. It tilted the entire axis of my existence in a single second.

I was Axl fucking Archer. Getting a chick pregnant was my fucking nightmare. The exact opposite of my modus operandi. My whole life, I'd done everything I could to avoid knocking chicks up. If I barebacked it, I spent the next couple weeks fuckin' sweating it out until the chick was on the rag again. And I always got lucky. Guess I figured I'd always be.

But when it came from Holly, it changed everything instantly. Her words filled me with a joy I couldn't describe, and from that moment on, I knew that I would do anything—any fucking thing—to protect that baby.

I rocketed up from the bench I sat on, expression breaking out into a massive grin the likes of which I hadn't displayed for weeks.

"Babe," I said, my voice rising in uncontrollable excitement, "You shittin' me?"

A smile slowly spread over her face, too. "No, Axl. I'm not shittin' you."

I wrapped one hand around her waist, stepped forward, and bent her backwards as I kissed her deeply. I felt more alive than I ever had before—this was a natural fuckin' high, with which the likes of booze, dope, and smokes couldn't compare.

I was kissing the mother of my child now, and it might've been the most goddamn romantic moment of my life.

I wanted to take her again right there, to fill her up with my seed again, to make fucking damn sure that she was pregnant. I wanted her fertile for me, wanted to claim her, breed her, wanted to own every inch of that gorgeous body.

How did a scumbag like me hook up with such a smart, beautiful girl?

When I finally broke our kiss and pulled away, we were both panting for air. I'd gone in to take the breath from her lungs, but she'd taken the breath from mine—just like she always did.

"Babe," I said, taking both her hands in mine, "That's the best news I've heard in forever."

Her expression was a mix of tenderness, happiness, and relief. "So you're happy?" she asked, shellshocked.

"Am I happy?" I laughed out loud. "Did you hear anything I just fuckin' said to you?"

She grinned wide, and I did too. I just stood there like a statue, holding her and looking into her eyes before I finally got ahold of myself.

I sat back down on the edge of the bench, slowly running a hand through my thick hair, trying to contemplate what this meant for me—for us.

"I can't do this with a baby on the way," I said, half under my breath.

Holly exhaled sharply, then sat down next to me on the bench. She put an arm around my shoulder and started rubbing it gently. I placed a hand on her thigh. God, I wanted her so bad, but I felt a new instinct, one that I didn't know I was capable of. I wanted her, but my need to protect and provide for her first had intensified a thousand times.

"Axl," she said, "Will you walk away from it all?"

Her words took me out of my trance, the fleeting moment of total bliss gone, as I remembered the fucked-up situation that we were in.

I shook my head slowly. "Babe," I said, "I'd do anything for you. For this baby. And I will. But this score has gotta be settled."

"So not anything," she said.

"You're askin' me to do the one thing I can't," I said. "Look. I'm outta the club now. Couldn't go back even if I wanted. But Lynch and Dash gotta pay. That's somethin' I just can't walk away from."

She took her arm off my shoulder, and crossed her arms in front of her. Fuck. How short-lived that moment had been. Of course reality had to rear its ugly head and bite us both in the ass right away.

"So you still don't care if you come back alive?" she said.

I shook my head. Hard. "No, babe," I said. "The baby changes *everything* about that."

I was bein' as honest as I could. This mornin' I'd been prepared to walk right into the devil's nest, and I very well might've if I'd known that Holly would be safe when I was gone.

But a baby. I didn't fucking trust anyone else with my baby, and that meant I *had* to come back alive. Dash and Lynch would pay, but I needed a new plan. Needed to be smarter, craftier. Needed to set aside my recent suicidal tendencies and get my head straight.

"So what're you gonna do?" Holly asked. "Those men want you dead, and they're never gonna let their guard down now."

"That's where I might've been fuckin' wrong," I said, thinking. "Dash left me for dead in that house. He thinks I'm six feet under right now."

"You have the element of surprise," she said.

"Yeah," I said. I'd been planning to use that element of surprise when I busted straight into the Sons clubhouse, like a skeleton risen from the dead. But maybe there was a smarter way to use it.

"What about the Reapers?" asked Holly.

Again, the gears in my head were turning, the pistons firing smoothly. The plan was coming together in my mind, just like it always did when I needed it to.

I stared into space, processing the details of the plan forming in my mind. "I'll feed 'em to each other," I said. "This shit started 'cause of a deal with the devil. It'll end the same way."

Holly looked worried. "What do you mean?"

"The Reapers want Lynch dead," I said. "*Need* him dead. He's masterminding the Sons strikes against 'em, killed more than a dozen by now. He's their most wanted man. And I'm gonna deliver him straight to 'em."

"What about Dash?" she asked.

I tightened my lips, fury pouring out of my heart. "Dash," I said, "I'll deal with myself."

CHAPTER 38: HOLLY

"Gonna need your help for this," Axl said, sitting next to me on the bench. "You got another camera?

"No," I said. "I saved for a year to buy mine. Before you destroyed it."

He coughed. "Damn. Any way to get another one?"

"Hmm," I thought out loud. "I can borrow equipment at school. If they haven't deactivated my student ID." I'd missed finals, and grades would be posted anytime now. I had no idea if I'd still be enrolled after missing all of my exams.

"Can you mic me up? Like a wire under my jacket?"

I thought for a moment. "Yeah," I said. "Shouldn't be difficult. Are you gonna tell me what this is about?"

"You're gonna do some film work for me."

"Elaborate?"

"You filmed Vargas once. Need you to do it again, just like last time."

"Well, it better not be *just* like last time," I said.

"Nah, it won't be," said Axl, putting an arm around my shoulders. "Do you think I'd let anything happen to you?"

"No," I said, truthfully.

"Then trust me."

I swallowed hard and nodded.

"Aright," Axl said. "Let's go for a ride."

Axl borrowed a spare bike from Big Mikey and we hit the road. It was nearly a five hour ride to SAU, but it felt good to be on a bike again. Instead of in a cage, as Axl called it.

When we got to my school, my ID still opened the film department doors—thank god. I checked out the equipment Axl asked for—a new camera and a couple microphones. We got back on the road and returned to the NOMAD compound. It was after dark by the time we arrived and my ass was killing me.

"Figure out how to mic me up tonight," said Axl as he took his helmet off. "Then we hit the road before light tomorrow."

Axl pulled out his cell phone and dialed. I wondered who he was calling, but I didn't have to wonder for long.

"Vargas," he said grimly. "You know who this is."

Vargas's voice in the speaker spoke faintly, but I couldn't make out the words. He sounded hostile as hell, whatever he was saying.

"Need you to meet me down at the Saguaro Junction tomorrow," said Axl. "Yeah. 8am sharp. No, just me. Bring whoever you want. Yes. I'm fucking serious."

He hung up. "We've got a date tomorrow."

It was a restless night for us both, and we got up around five, before the sun rose. We headed out to the Junction on Axl's bike, the frigid morning wind stinging our skin.

The Junction turned out to be nothing more than an isolated rest stop with a bathroom and an old visitor's center that resembled a gazebo with windows. It was still pitch black outside when we dismounted the bike, and Axl pulled a flashlight out of the bike's saddlebag. He shined it on the small, freestanding visitor center. But the beam of light stopped against the glass, and I couldn't see what was inside.

"One-way glass," said Axl, walking toward the structure. I followed. behind him, carrying the camera I'd checked out. "We're gonna post you up in this bitch. Need you to get *everything* on camera," he said. "You're sure this'll pick up the audio?" he asked, motioning to the mic I'd set up under his jacket.

I nodded. "Yes."

"Then let's get you situated in here. Soon as you see Vargas and his cronies roll up, hit it."

Axl returned to the bike and got a crowbar from the saddlebag, then returned to the door of the visitor's center where I stood. He started to pry it open.

Finally, the door popped open with a crunch. Axl shined the light inside. It was empty, abandoned, containing nothing more than a chair and a bunch of cobwebs. "Get cozy," said Axl. He chucked the crowbar down into the corner, where it bounced off the ground with a clang. "Never wanna see another one of those," he said. "You good?"

I nodded. "I'll start on your signal," I said. "Be careful." I stuck my neck out and planted a kiss on his cheek, his thick, wiry beard scraping my lips. He kissed me back on the lips, filling me full of warmth. "This'll be over quick, darlin'," he said. He walked out, pulling the door shut behind him.

I brushed the dust off the old chair and sat down. I mounted the camera on my shoulders, turned on the audio monitor on my headset, and waited.

The sun eventually came up, and just like clockwork, a fleet of motorcycles pulled up right before eight o'clock. I heard Axl's voice in my headset. "Go," he said. I hit the red record button with my thumb, and the camera started. I framed the scene with the viewfinder and waited as the bikes came to a stop.

I recognized Vargas by his sheer size as he dismounted his bike and approached Axl. I zoomed in on the two of them.

"Archer," came Vargas's voice over the mic. "This'd better be fucking good." Then he added, "The hell happened to you?"

"That's why I'm here," said Axl, pointing to his face. "The Sons did this to me."

Vargas snickered. "Nice club you got," he said.

"Just two of 'em," Axl replied. "And one of 'em is Lynch."

Vargas's face reddened visibly in the camera's viewfinder. "That sonofabitch's killed a dozen of my guys."

"I know. You want him dead."

"Goddamn right I do."

"Then we have a mutual interest."

"What're you sayin'?" asked Vargas, his eyes narrowing.

"I'll lead him into your arms. Lynch'll be all yours," said Axl, "But the other one who'll be with him, you gotta turn over to me. It's personal."

"Why the hell would I trust you?" said Vargas. He stepped closer to Axl, but Axl didn't back down. "I've killed so many of the fuckin' dogs in your club. I think you're settin' me up," he growled.

"Stop the tape and come out," said Axl. I heard Vargas bark in surprise as I switched the camera off and came out around the building.

The half-dozen Reapers saw me instantly, with the camera on my shoulder.

"Guess you gotta trust me now, motherfucker," came Axl's voice through my headset. "Just got your murder confession on tape."

One of the men standing behind Vargas darted out around him, heading straight for me. But Axl turned and plowed his balled-up fist straight into the guy's temple, and he went down hard.

"Know what a cloud upload is?" said Axl. "Try that shit one more time, and the video goes straight to the Feds."

I cringed. That was a bluff. The camera was totally not hooked up to the Internet. I couldn't even send a damn text out here. But it was apparently a good enough bluff for an old crony like Vargas.

"Alright, alright," growled Vargas, motioning for his men to stand down. "We do this your way. But when it's over, that video is gone. You rat on me," he said, holding his fist out toward Axl, "You and your old camera lady there ain't *never* gonna be safe."

"Agreed. You help me round up Lynch and Dash, I scrub the video. You'll have the upper hand in the war against the Sons, and you'll never hear from me again."

Axl held out his hand to shake, but Vargas just stepped back and spit in the dirt. "I better not," he said.

Axl shrugged and put his arm back down at his side. "Tomorrow, one p.m.," he said. "Be at Exit 74. Bring traffic spikes. And for fuck's sake, wait for the first bike to pass before you throw 'em down," he said, "Cause that'll be me."

CHAPTER 39: AXL

I slept in Holly's bed at the NOMAD compound that night, and woke up the next morning fired up.

The golden morning sun streamed in through the cracks in the blinds, illuminating Holly's skin. It was so precious, so delicate, almost translucent in the light. I ran a hand down her neck, over her breasts, feeling her soft nipples under her tank top as she slept. Then I slid my hand down to her belly, and held it gently. That was my future kid in there, and no way was I gonna let my future kid grow up without two parents. No way was I gonna let him or her end up like a lost, wandering feral kid like me.

Holly stirred, her eyes fluttering open. She looked up at me and smiled wistfully. "You ready for this, babe?" She asked.

"Never been more ready," I said. Confidence and determination surged through my body.

"We're outta here when it's done, right?"

"We're outta here," I send, bending down to kiss her on the forehead. "You stay put here where you're safe. I'll be back before you know it." I squeezed her hand and got out of bed.

It was fucking go time.

The key to all this was that today was the Sons' monthly arms pickup with the Russians. It always happened in the same place—a valley about a mile and a half off Exit 74.

Lynch and Dash would be there. They always were. And I was gonna lead those cunts right into the Reapers' arms.

Never fuckin' thought in a million years it'd come to this. Going up against my own club. But I knew now, that in this life, no matter how much control I thought I had, it was all an illusion. There was no such thing as control in this life. All I could do was respond to the fucked-up curveballs it threw at me. And sometimes, they were *really* fucked up.

I geared up, putting on a set of heavy leathers. I threw an extended mag into my Glock, and two more on my belt.

I was gonna need 'em.

The pickup always happened at high noon. I headed out an hour early. I had to be there and in position before either club showed.

As I left the NOMAD compound, I passed a guy in the hall I hadn't seen before. He wore leathers, but no patches.

"Ride safe, man," he said to me with a smirk as I passed him. I whirled around to speak, but he kept walking.

Fucking sketched me out for some reason, but I trusted Big Mikey. He vetted everyone who came in here, and he was doing double security duty now.

Still, I doubled back to Holly's room, going the opposite direction of the man. When I got there, I cracked the door. She was sleeping soundly.

"Be back soon," I whispered. I locked the door from the inside and closed it. Then I headed out of the compound.

I got to the drop-off point on time. It was an old warehouse in a valley off the side of the road, secluded from view of the main highway. The hills surrounding the valley were thick with desert brush—a perfect place to hide my bike. I roared up the dusty hills, praying not to get a flat as my bike climbed the dirt-and-brush road. Eventually I got to the top of the hill and killed the engine.

Looking down, I had a perfect view of the valley and warehouse below. But anyone down there wouldn't be able to see me up on the hill, obscured by the vegetation.

I grabbed my canteen off my bike and sat down. I closed my eyes and drank as I waited.

Twenty minutes later, I heard the rumble of bikes.

The Sons got there first. I squinted, looking down at who'd come. Looked like Ryker, with his unmistakeable ponytail, Dash, Lynch, Sandbag, a prospect, and four men I didn't recognize.

I pulled my Glock off my belt, pulled the slide back, and released it. A golden glint flickered through the ejection port as a round entered the chamber.

Then, I leveled my gun at the warehouse below. I aimed squarely for the building, not the men—I wanted these fuckers alive. Then, I pulled the trigger over and over until I emptied the mag. Each blast was defeating, and my eardrums burned over and over with pain, the loud cracks striking my eardrums.

The men below scrambled for cover, grabbing guns off their own belts.

I cupped my hands against my mouth. "On the ground!" I bellowed, my distinctive, deep voice booming over the valley.

Of course, I didn't expect those fuckers to lay down and die. The sound of my voice would be the only thing Dash and Lynch needed to hear, and they'd be after me like hyenas.

I jammed the Glock in its holster, ran to my bike, and started the engine. Voices and the roar of bikes drifted up from the valley. It was now or never.

I thundered down the side of the dirt hill, the bike bucking wildly up and down, the suspension being jarred by every pothole and rock in the road. I held onto the handlebars for dear life, almost being thrown the fuck off into the prickly pear cactus that dotted the mountain.

When I hit the bottom of the hill, I stuck out my foot, turning the bike sharply, and heading for the highway. Just as I pulled up onto the road, I spotted two bikes in pursuit.

Dash and Lynch. Just as I'd expected.

I popped the clutch and twisted the throttle as hard as it'd go. The 1500cc engine between my legs rocketed to life, and I felt the g-forces build against my chest as I launched onto the highway, Dash in Lynch in hot pursuit.

At that speed, it only took a little over a minute to get to Exit 74, but it felt like an hour.

It was now or never. Vargas's guys would either be there, or I was fucking screwed.

I came around the final bend, twisting the throttle all the way until it stopped. I shot past Exit 74, twisting my head to look over my shoulder.

Four guys with Reaper jackets ran out from behind the hills on either side of the road, throwing spike strips out across the highway.

Dash and Lynch didn't have a chance to hit the brakes. Their bikes thundered over the spike strips, and four loud pops echoed over the hills as their tires punctured and deflated. Behind them, a group of Reaper bikes roared to life, pulling up beside them and boxing them in. The entire fleet slowed down and came to a stop, Dash and Lynch unable to go any further on their flattened tires.

I hit the brakes hard, coming to a full stop. I executed a u-turn and slowly rejoined the group on the highway.

Energy surged through my body, down my legs, up my spine. I fuckin' had them.

Reapers piled off their bikes, rushing up to Dash and Lynch. They pulled the pair off their bikes and threw them to the ground. Everything according to plan.

Then, something happened that I didn't expect.

Another bike came down the highway. But it wasn't Ryker, or the prospect.

It was the man I'd seen at the compound earlier.

And on the back of his fucking bike, was Holly, with a gag in her mouth.

CHAPTER 40: HOLLY

Unable to hold onto the bike with my tied hands, I squeezed my legs together for dear life, trying to glue myself to the tiny passenger seat beneath me.

I'd been dozing in the early morning when I'd been awakened by a terrifying cracking noise. My eyes flew open just in time to see a burly, leather-clad figure enter my room, cross the room quick as a bullet, and stuff a hand over my mouth.

The next half hour had been a blur. The man covered me with a blanket, snuck me out of the compound, and threw me on the back of his bike.

Where we were going, I did not know until we got there.

As we approached Exit 74, I saw that the road was completely blocked by a mess of bikes and bikers. Two bikes were tipped over, and their riders lay on the ground, pinned down by other men.

Axl stood over them, next to Vargas. Even from a distance, I could see the shock and horror on his face as he saw us approaching.

As soon as the bike stopped, my kidnapper yanked me off the bike. He wrapped an arm around my neck from behind, and with the other hand, held a gun to my temple.

Inside, I felt surprisingly calm. This wasn't the first time I'd been stolen from my bed. *Stay cool,* I told myself, *it's your best chance to survive.*

"Lynch," my captor bellowed, "She's here!" He rammed the steel barrel of his revolver into my temple, and I instinctively rolled my neck to the side to stop the pain. But he just pushed harder. "Let him up," he shouted, "Let Lynch up!"

We stood only about ten yards away from Axl, and I could see his face clearly. He gritted his teeth before speaking. "Let 'im up," he growled.

The men holding Lynch down released their grips. Lynch, his face red and raw and his jeans now tattered, stood up. The pained look on his face told me that he'd been injured.

He staggered toward us, his right leg limping as he tried to keep his knee straight. "Give me the girl," he said. His voice was thick with hatred and madness.

Lynch grabbed me out of the man's hands, and put me in a headlock between his elbow and ribs. I stumbled over his feet as he squeezed my neck tight. He bent down, producing a knife from a sheath in his boot. He held it against the side of my neck, and my skin prickled at the touch of cold steel. I fought to keep my balance, to not fall over. I had to keep the baby safe at all costs.

"Archer," Lynch snarled, "Stubborn son of a bitch, ain't you? You shoulda died when you had the chance. Now it's your old lady's turn."

I screamed under the gag, wrenching my body sideways, channeling all my strength as I tried to force myself out of

Lynch's grip. But it was no use. I couldn't get the leverage I needed to break free.

"Lynch," said Axl, stepping forward, "This ain't about her. Never was. This is between you and me."

"Don't worry, VP, I'll put flowers on her grave," said Lynch nastily. I couldn't see his face, but I swear his tone of voice betrayed a smile on his face.

"I'm outta the club," said Axl. "You're VP now. Just let her go."

Dash was still lying on the ground, struggling against the men who pinned him down. Lynch had been loyal to him only as long as he'd been useful. Now, Dash lay on the asphalt, useless and forgotten.

"You *are* outta the club," said Lynch, scraping the edge of his knife against my cheek. "But it ain't good enough. I wanna see you bleed."

"Make me bleed then. Leave the woman out of it, you fucking coward."

Lynch snarled with animal rage, releasing me and pushing me down to the ground in one motion. I twisted my body as I fell, cushioning the impact with my side. My only thought was to protect the baby growing inside my belly.

I watched the scene unfold from the ground. Lynch charged at Axl, holding the knife out at him in a reverse grip. No one in the Reaper crew moved to intervene. It was a matter of street honor, I knew. A beef between two men. They were prepared to let it play out how it may. Frankly, the Reapers would've been happy to let the two men tear each other to shreds.

But it didn't play out that way. Lynch never had a chance. As he flew toward Axl, raising the knife for one, final, fatal stroke, Axl swung out of the way. He kicked out with a heavy boot, clipping Lynch right on his injured knee. The knife flew out of his hands as he crashed to the asphalt on his back, clattering away harmlessly.

Axl crashed down on top of Lynch, sitting on his stomach and pressing a forearm down into his neck.

Lynch made agonized, gasping noises as he struggled to breathe. With his other hand, Axl reached out and snagged the handle of Lynch's knife, pulling it within reach. He wrapped his fist around the handle and brought it to Lynch's throat.

"This is for betraying me," said Axl. He plunged the knife into Lynch's throat, and Lynch's gasping instantly turned to a gurgle.

"And this," said Axl, his face deadly, "is for Holly." His elbow jerked as he twisted the knife in Lynch's throat.

A fountain of blood sprayed out of Lynch's throat, coloring the asphalt dark red. Two or three seconds later, he lay completely silent and motionless, blood flowing out of his neck like a river.

Axl stood up, wiping his forehead off with the arm of his jacket. He left the knife jutting out of Lynch's throat.

I rolled onto my back and managed to sit up. Vargas walked toward Axl.

"Damn," he said. "The deal was for Lynch alive, motherfucker."

Axl eyed Vargas warily. "He left me no choice."

Vargas looked hard at Axl, and then smiled his creepy smile. "Just shittin' you. We good, Archer." He laughed and clapped Axl on the shoulder. "Hell of a show." He turned to a couple of his guys behind him. "Clean that shit up."

Axl hurried over to me and pulled the gag out of my mouth before pulling me off the ground. He pulled out his own knife and cut the ties around my hands.

"Axl," I said in relief, "It's finally over." I didn't have a doubt left in the world that this man would do anything it took—absolutely anything—to protect me and the baby.

"Almost," he said, pulling away from my embrace. "There's one more thing."

He looked down at Dash.

CHAPTER 41: AXL

"Axl, man, what are you doing?" Dash whined. He struggled, his hands cuffed behind him around a thick metal pipe. The metal-on-metal clanging echoed through the abandoned warehouse. The only other sounds were our breathing and the faint whistle of wind moving through cracked windows and walls. The heat inside the warehouse was sweltering, the air static and unmoving.

"Shut up," I said, staring into his eyes. "You sound fucking pathetic."

On my orders, the Reapers had loaded Dash into their chase van and brought us back down the road to the warehouse. There was no sign of the other Sons or the Russians. They'd probably seen Lynch and Dash fall into the Reaper trap and split. That was cool with me. I didn't want to fucking go up against any more Sons. I wished no ill toward Ryker and the rest of them.

It was just me and Dash in here. Lynch was fucking history. And now it was time to finish the job. Time to administer payback for the near-lethal beating and betrayal I'd gotten.

It was time for justice.

"Come on, man," said Dash, his voice sounding increasingly urgent and pathetic. "It was just business, man. You know what happens to guys who betray the club."

I snarled out loud and spit in his face. "The only one of us who betrayed this club is you," I said. "You wanna get a man out? Fucking Mayhem vote. Then finish 'em off honorably. Don't fucking bash 'em on the head and leave 'em to die. Goddamn fool."

"Ryker never woulda gone for a Mayhem vote on you. You've always been his favorite. We were just protecting the club, man."

"Then the Sons have lost their way," I said. "I saw that the instant Ryker was willing to sacrifice Holly for convenience. Fuck the charter, right? Forget "No innocents die," right?"

"It's complicated—" began Dash, but I cut him off.

"It's the simplest fucking thing in the world," I said. "It's only complicated for weasel fuckers like you who try to rationalize everything."

"What're you gonna do?" asked Dash. Beads of sweat ran down his forehead. There were white streaks where past droplets had dried, leaving behind only salt.

That's what I wanted to happen to Dash. For him to disappear, leaving nothing more than a trail of white powder.

I sighed, stepping backwards from him. I pulled my Glock out of its holster, hitting the mag release with my thumb. The empty magazine slid out of the gun and fell to the concrete floor with a thud. I reached around and pulled a fresh mag from my belt, loading the gun and racking the slide back. Dash's eyes followed the gun, in fear and desperation.

"Sean," I said, using Dash's real name, "You remember when I first joined the Sons?"

He gulped and nodded.

"Remember how you always had my back? How you showed me the ropes?"

He nodded again.

"And how when I patched in, we cut our palms and mixed our blood that day? We were supposed to become blood brothers."

He started to speak, but I silenced him with a wave of the gun. "Don't fucking tell me this is just business," I said. "All my life, I bounced from place to place. Never fit in anywhere, 'til it came to this club. And this's how it ends. Attempted murder by my own brother."

Dash just looked down at his feet. He seemed to sag down, his legs giving up. "Make it quick," he said.

I raised my Glock in the air, and lined up the sights with his forehead. I put my finger on the trigger and began to squeeze, feeling the trigger spring reaching the point of no return.

In my mind, I saw Holly's face. She was waiting for me outside the warehouse. One jerk of my finger and this would all be over with, and we'd leave this shit life for something better.

I imagined what she'd think if she were on the other side of the wall, in here with me.

I thought about what she'd said about the cycle of violence in the club. How one violent act inevitably lead to another... and another... and another.

I thought of all the faces of the men I'd killed. 12 in total. I never forgot a single one of their faces.

And I thought about the baby growing inside Holly. A new life, a new hope for something better than the past. How I wanted a different life for that baby than what I'd had myself.

I felt the trigger begin to break under my finger... and then I stopped. I relaxed my finger and brought the gun down to my side.

Dash looked at me. "The fuck you waiting' for? Do it already!"

I looked and him and shook my head with contempt. But mixed with that contempt, there was forgiveness, something that I hadn't felt for a long time.

I jammed the Glock into my belt and walked up to him. I pulled the key to his handcuffs out of my pocket and freed him from the pipe.

He rubbed his wrists and eyed me suspiciously. "The fuck are you doing?"

I motioned with my head toward a pile of wooden crates in the corner of the warehouse. "Get the fuck over there," I said, "and don't come out until we're all far away from here."

"Why are you doing this?" asked Dash.

"Because," I said, "You ain't worth the fuckin' bullet it'd take to kill you. I don't ever want to hear from you again. Never come anywhere near me or my family. Don't even fuckin' think about me. I ever see your ugly face again, you die."

I waited for Dash to slink off into the corner of the warehouse. He sat behind a wooden crate, looking at the wall. He didn't turn around.

Satisfied that he wouldn't ambush me again, I walked out of the warehouse, and into the sunlight.

CHAPTER 42: HOLLY

When Axl emerged from the warehouse, the Reapers honored their truce with Axl. "Archer," said Vargas, "You fucking burn that tape into ashes, understand me?" Axl nodded. "Done."

We went our separate ways, the Reapers most likely heading to plot their next move against the Sons in their turf war, now that the Sons had lost their main general. The Sons had a chink in their armor now, and the Reapers would drill into it ruthlessly like they always did, trying to get to the soft meat underneath. As I knew now, any weakness was a sign to attack.

In this lifestyle, the shit never ended. But I knew now how strong its pull was. How this life sucked you in like quicksand, every path seeming to lead back to violence. Once you got sucked in, everything changed. Your choices were no longer your own; they were dictated by your enemies. You had to respond with strength, with resolve... with violence. If you didn't, you were dead.

I used to wonder why people couldn't work out their differences peacefully. My time in the club lifestyle taught

197

me why—because violence only causes more violence. And I used to think that Axl was the one who truly had freedom out here on his bike. But the truth was, he didn't really have any freedom at all. Not until he walked away from the club.

As we rode away from the warehouse, I asked Axl, "What did you do to Dash?"

He just replied, "We won't be hearing from him again." I didn't press him further.

That day, we said goodbye to Arizona forever. Axl never got his old bike back from the Sons, so the first thing we did when we left the NOMAD compound was hit a bike dealership.

We stood looking at the rows of cruisers and hogs, and I saw the excitement in Axl's eyes as he contemplated a new bike. One of my hands held his, and the other I held against my belly as we walked through the rows of bikes. The sun was beginning to go down, the sweltering heat giving way to a cool breeze.

Axl surprised me at the bike dealership. I thought for sure he would call the salesman over and say, "that one," pointing to one of the many Harleys, and we'd be on our way. But instead, after admiring them, he took me to the touring bikes.

"What do you think of this one?" he said, pointing to a big Honda touring bike. It was big, lumbering, and most of all, not dangerous looking at all. It had huge, wide seats, and big fairings to keep the wind off and make even the longest rides comfortable.

It was the kind of bike suitable for a growing family.

"I love it," I said, reaching up to plant a kiss on his lips. "But you're only allowed to ride this one on the weekends," I said, "at least until the baby comes. A bike is no place for a pregnant lady."

Axl grumbled to himself. "Bitches these days," he said to himself.

I punched him on the arm. "You're a real asshole."

Finally, a salesman came over to help us. A young guy, who honestly looked too clean-cut to be involved with motorcycles. But, I guessed that most of the dealership's customers were just old guys who drove four-door sedans to work every day, and took out their bikes on the weekends. A nice, clean-cut young guy like him was exactly the salesman they needed. A younger version of themselves.

"Sir, ridden one before?"

Axl glanced at me and we both grinned. "Yeah."

"Great, and do you have a motorcycle endorsement on your license?"

Axl nodded. "I do."

The salesman's face lit up. "In that case, you're welcome to take any of 'em for a spin. Insurance covers it!" Then he added, looking at Axl's inked arms, "Man, you sure could pass for a biker."

Axl laughed. "Maybe in another life," he said. He was joking with the guy, but I knew exactly what he meant.

"I don't need a test drive," he said. "That's the one I want."

The salesman looked surprised but didn't argue. "You got it, sir. Let's step into my office to discuss financing options."

Axl waved his hand. "I'll pay cash."

I guess that was one of the... lingering benefits of Axl's time in the club. We had all the cash we'd ever need.

We signed a contract for the bike and bought new riding gear and helmets at the apparel shop. Axl looked at the sporty red nylon jackets, and almost took one off the rack.

199

"Nah," he said, changing his mind. "Not ready for that bullshit." He walked over to the leather section and picked up a handsome-looking black leather jacket, albeit one that was not covered in motorcycle gang patches. He grinned at me.

We rode away from the dealership, heading east on the highway until the sun set. Axl took us to a hotel—this time, one that had free cookies and coffee in the lobby instead of a grumpy old man behind bulletproof glass.

Once we were in the room, we laid down on the bed, exhausted. I rested my head on his chest, and he ran his fingertips over my back lightly.

"So where to?" he asked me.

"I want you to pick," I said, looking up at him.

"Always wanted to go to Texas," he said.

"Then Texas it is," I replied. "Can I bring my parents up there once in a while?"

"Of course," he said.

"And college?"

"I'll cover whatever you need to finish your degree."

I sighed. It was nice to be taken care of. I ran a hand up his stomach, feeling the rock-hard muscles underneath. I felt like I'd gone into hell's den, and come out the other side alive and stronger.

"Baby," I said, "I love you."

He grinned. "I don't know if I've ever said those words before. But," he paused, "I love you too."

"Baby," I said, "Make love to me."

And he did.

CHAPTER 43: AXL

When we said our vows to each other six months later, she looked so damn beautiful standing there in her dress. I always thought I was the hottest shit in the room, but after seeing her like that, I had to stop and wonder if I was handsome enough for *her*.

We brought her parents out for the wedding. Her dad went fucking nuts the first time he heard the news, but when he and I sat down for a man-to-man, and I told him about the new oil business I was goin' into, he warmed up to me real fast. Good guy, too. Gonna make a great grandad.

Hell, even Ryker and I settled up our differences and he came on out. I guess some ties are stronger than blood. Big Mikey came too. Those two were the closest I ever had to a family, until I met Holly.

We found out that the baby's gonna be a boy. Didn't fuckin' dare say so, but goddamn was I relieved to hear that. Me raise a little girl? Jesus. I'd have a fuckin' coronary every time she left the house.

Speaking of houses. I got us a real nice place out by the panhandle. Similar enough to Arizona to feel like home, but far enough away to let bygones be bygones. It was a real big place, up on a hill by itself, with iron bars like the devil's claws. I ain't gonna hurt another man as long as I live... if I can help it. But should the day ever come, that someone comes lookin' for me, god help me, I will light that fucker up the instant he steps onto my property. I would kill again, but only for my girl and my boy.

I used to think I was the smartest motherfucker in the room. And well, that hasn't changed a damn bit. These oil execs I've been dealing with are easy pickings. They ain't got the toughness I do. But Holly taught me somethin' I dunno if I'd ever have figured out on my own. To respect life and to rise above. In the club life, everybody is down in the shit and there ain't no such thing as rising out of it. But on the outside, the sky's a little bluer, the birds a little cheerier.

I want a good life for my son. Not like the bullshit I went through. He can ride a bike when he's 18, yeah, but he'll wear a helmet and leathers. Not a skull cap, either, but one of those goofy fuckin' full-head cop helmets. On second thought... fuck that. My boy can ride fast and hard, 'cause he'll have the smarts and the reflexes to stay safe out there. Like me.

And as for Holly... shit. She's gettin' so big I swear she's gonna pop any minute, though the doc says it won't be for another few months. I just can't get enough of her. Her smell, her taste, her beautiful personality. Hard to fuckin' believe it all started out in the Coppertail junkyard. Thought I was gonna score with some hard cash back there, but what I ended up with was beyond my wildest dreams.

I heard through the grapevine that shit calmed down between the Sons and the Reapers. For now. I know how it is. Shit'll flare up again, and then blow over again, and on, and on, and on. That's how it works. How it always has, and how it always will.

So now I've got the money, the success, the woman, the looks, and a kid on the way. Posted up in the biggest state in the Union, with the biggest cock in the union. I can't wait to see what the future holds, 'cause I know it's gonna be bright for me. I got everything I need right here surrounding me, and I ain't ever gonna let 'em go.

Not on my life.

Thank You!

Love bad boy romances? Sign up for my no-spam mailing list to receive news on **new releases, free giveaways, and more!**

You can also join the advanced review team. I'm very much in need of people who are willing to read my books early and leave reviews upon release.

http://eepurl.com/bYD3Rv